Alex crouched lithely beside where she lay

Harriet felt a delicious coolness on her skin and realized that he was using sun lotion on her. She moved restively.

"Keep still," Alex ordered. "It's foolish falling asleep in the sun. You could have been badly burned."

She was burning now. As his hand stroked across her flesh, tiny fires were igniting all over her. And as his fingers moved downward, applying the lotion to her lower spine and the gentle curve of her hips above the line of her bikini briefs, she had to sink her teeth into the soft flesh of her lower lip to prevent herself from crying out.

What kind of a state was she in, that his lightest touch could produce such pleasure and such pain at the same time?

D0059728

SARA CRAVEN
is also the author of these

Harlequin Presents

and this

Harlequin Romance

Many of these books are available at your local bookseller.

For a free catalog listing all titles currently available,
send your name and address to:

HARLEQUIN READER SERVICE
1440 South Priest Drive, Tempe, AZ 85281
Canadian address: Stratford, Ontario N5A 6W2

SARA CRAVEN

pagan adversary

Harlequin Books

TORONTO • NEW YORK • LONDON
AMSTERDAM • PARIS • SYDNEY • HAMBURG
STOCKHOLM • ATHENS • TOKYO • MILAN

Harlequin Presents first edition August 1983
ISBN 0-373-10616-5

Original hardcover edition published in 1983
by Mills & Boon Limited

Printed in U.S.A.

CHAPTER ONE

'WHAT you're saying is that there's nothing I can do—that I can't win.' By a superhuman effort Harriet Masters kept her voice steady.

The man sitting opposite her at the wide, polished desk gave a slight shrug. 'You are mistaken if you regard this as a battle, Thespinis Masters. But if you insist on doing so, then I must tell you it is one you will find impossible to win. My client is prepared to carry his claim for custody of his nephew to any court either in this country or internationally. It would be a costly process, but one that he could afford. Whereas you——' he glanced down at some papers in front of him— 'You, I see, are a secretary.'

'Nothing so important,' Harriet said defiantly. 'I'm a typist. I earn a reasonable salary, but I can't fight the Marcos millions—I admit that. But my claim to Nicky is on moral grounds.' She took a deep breath. 'My sister was my only living relative. When she and Kostas married—when they had Nicky, they let me become part of their family. I—I even had a room in their house, and I was actually looking after Nicky when—when. . . .' She paused, struggling for composure.

'I am aware of that, *thespinis*,' Mr Philippides looked at her with a trace of compassion. 'It was a great tragedy, a grievous shock for you. But surely you wish for the best for the boy.'

Harriet returned his glance coolly. 'Naturally. But I think we differ on how we would interpret what's best for him.'

Mr Philippides pursed his lips. 'Come, *thespinis*.' There was a trace of impatience in his voice. 'In his uncle's care, he will have every possible advantage.'

'I'd find that easier to believe if that same uncle had

5

taken the slightest interest in him when he was born, and during the time before Kostas and Becca were— killed,' Harriet retorted, and was glad to see Mr Philippides look uncomfortable. In a detached way, she could almost feel sorry for him. He had a wretched job to do, and one that was probably little to his taste. But on the other hand, she thought cynically, Alex Marcos was undoubtedly paying him well to persuade her to hand little Nicky over without a struggle.

When she had arrived at the imposing suite of offices which housed the London branch of the Marcos corporation, she had been frankly terrified in case she had to face Alex Marcos himself. She had never met him, but Kostas naturally had spoken of him often, and although Harriet acknowledged that his view was coloured by the fact that there was little love lost between the brothers, there was no doubt that he sounded a formidable figure.

She had found Mr Philippides with his grizzled hair and rotund person a distinct relief, although she did not underestimate him. Anyone Alex Marcos employed would have high professional skills, and would be expected to win any encounters they undertook on his behalf.

But not this one, Harriet thought, her nails digging painfully into the palms of her hands. Not this one. I can't let Nicky go. He's all I have.

She stole a swift glance at herself in the huge mirror which dominated one wall of the office, and was glad to see that apart from a telltale spot of colour in each cheek, she looked relatively calm. She was thankful that Mr Philippides could not know how near collapse she had been through sheer tension as the lift had borne her swiftly upwards to the penthouse.

Alex Marcos' arrogant claim to Nicky had come as a complete shock to her. He and Kostas had been on cool terms for several years, and relations between them had been totally severed when Kostas married Becca against his family's wishes. From that moment on there had been no contact, either by letter or telephone, and Kostas had declared savagely that he would never go back to Greece again. Harriet could only be glad he had never known how tragically his prophecy would be fulfilled. He and Becca had been killed instantly on their way home from a friend's house when a car driven by a drunk had careered into their own vehicle at some crossroads.

From that moment, life had become a nightmare for Harriet, but she had coped with the inquest and the funeral because there was no one else to do it. And no one else to look after Nicky. The firm she worked for had allowed her several weeks leave with pay while she made what arrangements she could. The house had to be sold. It was on a mortgage, and she could not afford the payments. It was as much as she could do to pay the rent on the large bedsitter she had found. It was an airy room, but she had to share the kitchen and bathroom, and when Nicky grew older she would have to find something larger.

But she had been prepared for that. Prepared for all the eventualities and sacrifices that would be necessary, because she loved Nicky.

She had got him a place with a registered child-minder, a girl only a few years older than herself with twins of Nicky's age, and a pleasantly untidy house and garden. Manda Lane was a serene, unruffled personality and Harriet had taken to her immediately, and, what was more important, so had Nicky, who although too young to fully comprehend the rapid change in his circumstances, was nevertheless disturbed by it, and inclined to cling.

Life wasn't easy, and money was tight, but she was coping.

And then had come the letter from Alex Marcos' solicitors, informing her that he was claiming custody of his brother's child, and offering her payment in compensation.

She had been stunned by the letter's cruelty and

insensitivity, and had dashed off an impetuous refusal of his terms by return of post.

The next communication had been couched in slightly more conciliatory terms, but with no alteration in the basic demand. Nicky was to leave England and take up residence in Greece in his uncle's charge, and she, Harriet, was to relinquish all claims to him. Her reply to this showed no lessening of her own determination. There had been a lengthy pause, and she had begun to hope, idiotically, that Alex Marcos had thought better of engaging in what the media called a 'tug of love' over a child who was a total stranger to him.

He didn't need Nicky, she had persuaded herself. He had so much else—wealth, property, business interests which took him all over the world, and if the gossip columns were to be believed, more female company than was decent.

'We were born the wrong way round,' Kostas had said once ruefully. 'Alex is a wild man, a rover, a true pagan. That is the role of the young brother, *ne*? Whereas I—I am the tame, domesticated man. Very dull.'

He had laughed and looked at Becca, and something in their eyes and intimate smiles had brought a lump to Harriet's throat. There was nothing dull about their life together, she'd thought.

Led by her thoughts, aloud she said, 'Judging by what one reads in the papers, I'd have said Alex Marcos is the last man in the world to want to saddle himself with a small child. Won't it cramp his usual style?'

Mr Philippides almost gaped at her, and she saw with satisfaction that a faint film of perspiration had broken out on his swarthy forehead.

He said repressively, 'That is hardly a subject for discussion. You forget, *thespinis*, that the child Nicos is his heir.'

Harriet smiled. 'And he forgets that Nicky is my heir too.'

'*Po, po, po,*' Mr Philippides gestured impatiently. 'Let us speak seriously, Thespinis Masters, and practically too. What can you possibly hope to give the child in comparison to the Marcos family?'

'I can give him love,' Harriet said bravely. 'Nicky isn't a commodity, as Mr Marcos seems to think, judging by the insulting offer he made to me.'

Mr Philippides avoided her gaze 'That was perhaps—unfortunate.'

'That is putting it extremely mildly,' said Harriet.

Mr Philippides leaned forward. 'You must not mistake yourself, my dear young lady, that the child will not be cared for. As well as his uncle, his grandmother is also anxious to receive him.'

'What a pity they weren't equally anxious to receive my sister.' Harriet's tone held a note of steel.

She could remember Kostas' distress at the implacable silence which greeted his marriage. 'Mama and Alex!' he had raged. 'All my life I have taken their orders—obeyed them dutifully. But all that is forgotten now. In their eyes I have transgressed—and neither of them will forgive or forget.'

Harriet's heart muscles contracted at the thought of little Nicky growing up in such an atmosphere.

Mr Philippides sighed. 'It could hardly be expected they would welcome such a match,' he said, clearly making an effort to be placatory. 'You do not fully understand, dear young lady, that in our country such matters are often still arranged. A bride had already been chosen for the late Mr Marcos. His marriage to your sister caused great offence—deep embarrassment.'

'Then why didn't Alex marry her himself, if it was so important?' Harriet snapped. 'As for Nicky being his heir, that's a ridiculous argument. He's bound to marry and have children himself one day—if he can find any woman fool enough to tie herself up to him—and where will Nicky be then?' She thumped the desk with her clenched fist. 'He has—everything, Mr Philippides— and I only have Nicky. I won't give him up. If Mr Marcos wants him, he'll have to fight for him!'

'I hope that is not your final word, Thespinis Masters.' As Harriet rose to her feet, Mr Philippides stood up too.

'No,' said Harriet. 'My final word is—tyrant. A Greek word, I think. In England, we don't believe in them.'

She marched to the door without a backward glance.

Her bravado had faded slightly when she reached the street. In fact she was shaking so much, she had to pause for a few moments in the doorway until she had regained her self-control

The interview had not in fact taken as long as she had anticipated, and there was still nearly three-quarters of an hour left of her lunch break, although she had little appetite.

It was a fine sunny day, and several of the pubs she passed on her way back to her own office had awnings out, and tables on the pavement. Reasoning that she couldn't do a full afternoon's work on an empty stomach, no matter how churned-up that stomach might be, Harriet sat down at one of the outside tables, ordering a tomato juice and a cheese sandwich.

She might have promised Alex Marcos a fight, she thought sombrely, but Mr Philippides had been right when he said she could not win. He had everything going for him—money, power, resources. How could she hope to convince anyone, let alone a court of law, that she would be a more suitable guardian for a small child?

She sighed, and tossed the remains of a crust to a hopefully strutting pigeon.

Besides, couldn't it be argued that by attempting to keep Nicky, she was actually being selfish? She did want Nicky to have all the advantages that the Marcos family could provide, but she could not. Had she any real justification for depriving him of them?

She thought wistfully how lonely life would be

without Nicky. At just over two and a half, he was beginning to talk quite fluently, and enjoy the nursery rhymes and stories she read to him. The thought of losing that close and loving relationship for ever—of abandoning him to people who were strangers, who even spoke an alien language—chilled her to the bone.

If the relationship between Kostas and his brother had been a normal one, the situation could have been so different, she thought sadly. But the Marcos family had never even acknowledged Becca, and the feelings of her younger sister would have no significance at all in their reckonings. The fact that they had cynically offered her a sum of money to induce her to part with Nicky without a fuss proved how little they estimated her.

Poor Kostas, she thought. He had always been reticent on the exact nature of the quarrel which had driven him to England, away from his family, but if it was to escape an unwanted marriage with a comparative stranger, then it was quite understandable.

When he and Becca had met, it had been several months before he had even told her that he was related to the Marcos family. In fact their romance had nearly ended when Becca discovered the truth, because she felt almost overwhelmed by it. She was a gentle girl, and the jet-setting lifestyle of the man who was to be her brother-in-law repelled and frightened her. It took all the persuasion and all the assurances that Kostas was capable of to convince her that his was a very different personality.

Harriet suspected that the unconcealed hostility of the Marcos family to the marriage had almost come as a relief to Becca. Kostas was working as an accountant and earning sufficient to provide for their needs, and that was all she wanted.

Harriet sighed. If only Alex Marcos or his mother had seen them together, she thought passionately, had seen how much they loved each other, then they must have relented. But at the same time, a small cold voice deep inside her told her that she was being sentimental. A man as ruthlessly successful as Alex Marcos would regard any such change of heart as a sign of weakness.

She got up, brushing a few stray crumbs from her navy pleated skirt, and began to walk along the street, not hurrying, looking into the windows of shops she passed with unseeing eyes.

There was a danger, and she could see it, of making Nicky the centre of her world. She rarely went out now in the evenings. For one thing, baby-sitters cost money, but more importantly it seemed wrong not to spend as much time as possible with Nicky at the only time it was possible—after work. She had never grudged him one minute of her time, or felt deprived, but sometimes when she heard the other girls she worked with chatting animatedly about boy-friends and outings, she felt as if she occupied another world.

At twenty-one, she was hardly likely to be written off as a spinster, the archetypal maiden aunt, she knew. She wasn't conceited, but she was aware that her pale fair hair and wide grey eyes had an attraction all their own. But she also knew that Nicky's existence in her life was a drawback as far as men were concerned. Roy, for instance.

She flushed slightly as she remembered that she had actually been considering becoming engaged to Roy. Then the accident had happened, and her life had changed overnight, and somehow Roy wasn't there any more. She'd been bewildered, and more than a little hurt, because she had counted on his support. But he had been almost brutally frank.

'I'm sorry, love,' he'd said, 'but I didn't bargain for a ready-made family. I don't want to have to share your attention with a kid who isn't even my own.'

Harriet had told herself she was well rid of him, and knew that it was true, but the hurt still lingered, and made her chary of accepting such invitations that did come her way.

Claudia who occupied the adjoining desk at the office

pool was always trying to make dates for her, and urging her to go out more, insisting that she owed it to herself. But Harriet felt that it was Nicky who was owed—owed as settled and secure an environment as she could create for him, at least for the time being.

Claudia was waiting agog for her return. 'What happened?' she hissed.

Harriet shrugged. 'We talked. I lost my temper.'

Claudia grinned. 'It's amazing,' she said. 'You are the image of a cool blonde, and yet it's like an ice-cap over a volcano. Was it the great man himself?'

Harriet shook her head, and Claudia made a frustrated noise.

'Damn, there goes my last chance of finding out what a really sexy man is like! I expected you to come reeling back here with stars in your eyes and no buttons left on your blouse.'

'You're joking, of course.' Harriet was acid.

'Not really,' Claudia grinned. 'After all, he must have something. Look at the birds he pulls!'

Harriet smiled cynically as she wound papers and carbons into her typewriter. 'Oh, he's got something all right,' she agreed. 'Money.'

Claudia snorted. 'Bet it's more than that. Haven't you ever seen a photograph of him?'

Harriet shrugged. 'The odd newspaper one. But they don't tell you much except he hasn't got two heads. It's a pity he hasn't, really,' she added thoughtfully, 'then everyone would know what a monster he is.'

'Miss Masters!' The typing pool supervisor materialised beside Harriet's desk, looking severe. 'Miss Greystoke has buzzed. You're wanted in the chairman's suite.'

Harriet's fingers stilled on the keys of her machine. She was a good efficient worker, and she had sometimes taken dictation for the managing director and the company secretary when their own girls were away, but the chairman was another kettle of fish altogether. None of the typing pool ever filled in for the remote and efficient Miss Greystoke. And anyway, if Miss Greystoke had buzzed, it was reasonable to suppose that she was there, and not requiring a substitute.

'When you're quite ready, Miss Masters,' the supervisor reminded her sarcastically.

The chairman's suite and the other executive offices were one floor up, and Harriet walked up the stairs, trying to tuck errant strands of hair back into the smooth coil she wore on top of her head. What on earth could Sir Michael want her for? she wondered in alarm. In the two years she had been with the company, she had never even spoken to him. When Kostas and Becca had been killed, it had been the company secretary Mr Crane who had dealt with her, and he had been kindness himself. But perhaps Sir Michael didn't think she was worth the time and the money she had been allowed. But if so, was it likely he would summon her to tell her so himself?

She was totally mystified by the time she reached Miss Greystoke's office. Miss Greystoke was looking at her watch ostentatiously when she knocked politely and went in.

'At last,' she said coolly. 'You're to go straight in.'

'Yes.' Harriet hesitated. 'Do—do you know by any chance what it's about?'

Miss Greystoke looked as if she was about to be withering, then suddenly relented, perhaps noticing for the first time Harriet's pallor.

'I haven't the slightest idea. There was a message waiting when I got back from lunch.' She smiled. 'But don't look so worried. He's not a bad old stick, you know,' she added, lowering her voice.

Harriet returned the smile nervously. She walked over to the door of the inner office, squared her shoulders resolutely, pressed the handle down and went in.

Unlike Miss Greystoke's office, which was artificially lit, the chairman's room had windows the length of one wall, and the sudden glare of sunlight almost dazzled Harriet as she stood hesitating, just inside the door.

For a moment, all she was aware of was a man's figure standing at one of the windows, and then as he turned and came towards her, she realised in an odd panic that whoever this was, it wasn't Sir Michael.

For one thing, this man was at least twenty years his junior, black-haired with a dark, harshly attractive face. He was tall too, and expensive tailoring did full justice to the breadth of his shoulders and his lean hips and long legs.

Harriet took a breath. 'I'm sorry—there's been some mistake,' she began, backing towards the door.

He held up a swift authoritative hand, halting her.

'Oh, don't run away, Miss Masters.' His voice was as harsh as his face, with a faint foreign intonation. 'You were brave enough to my lawyer not so long ago. What do you dare say to my face, I wonder?'

Oh no, Harriet thought in anguish. It can't be true! It can't be him.

Trying to sound cool, she said, 'Am I supposed to know who you are?'

'We'll dispense with the games, if you please,' he said. 'We're both well aware of each other's identity.'

Harriet swallowed. 'How—how did you know where I work?'

'I know everything I need to know about you,' he said cuttingly. 'Including the fact that you are not a fit person to be in charge of my brother's child.'

Harriet gasped. 'You have no right to say that!'

'I have every right,' he said. 'Every word you said to Philippides revealed your immaturity, your headstrong foolishness. You destroyed any case you might have had for retaining Nicos in your care with your own silly tongue.'

'Mr Philippides didn't waste any time in making a full report,' she said furiously. 'Did he use a tape recorder?'

'No, Miss Masters. I saw and heard you myself.' He

paused. 'The mirror in that room has another function apart from allowing young girls to preen themselves in it.'

A two-way mirror. Harriet had only heard of such things.

She said, 'That's the most despicable thing I've ever heard!'

'But then your experience had been so limited.'

'No wonder your brother was glad to get away from you,' she said recklessly, and halted, appalled at the expression of molten rage on his face.

She said in a voice that didn't sound like her own. 'I—I didn't mean that.'

'I should hope not.' His face was grim.

Harriet made a little helpless movement with her hands. 'I don't think you understand how upset I've been—about Nicky. He's all I have in the world.'

'At present, perhaps,' he agreed. 'Apart from the fact that you have a tongue like a shrew, you shouldn't find it hard to attract a husband, particularly with the money I have offered you as a dowry.'

Harriet's newly acquired cool went up in smoke. 'I wouldn't touch a penny of your bloody money!'

'Your language is unbecoming,' he said icily. 'If you think to force me into making a higher offer by your intransigence, then forget it. You're not worth what I have already suggested, but I wish to have the matter settled quickly. The child's grandmother wishes to see him.'

'The child's grandmother could have had every opportunity of seeing him over the past two years.' Harriet's voice shook.

'Was that what your sister counted on?' he asked. 'That the birth of her child would give her the entrée into our family? How mistaken she was! Let me advise you not to fall into the same error, Miss Masters, of playing for stakes that are beyond you. You will only lose.'

She took two hasty steps forward, her hand swung up, and she slapped him hard across his face.

The sound was like a shot going off in the quiet room, and it was followed by a terrifying silence. Harriet stood in horror, watching the marks of her fingers appear across his swarthy cheek. She saw an almost murderous flare in his eyes and braced herself for some kind of retaliation, to be shaken perhaps, or slapped in her turn, but none came.

At last he said, 'Violent as well as insolent. What have you to say now?'

She said, 'If you're waiting for me to apologise, then you'll wait for ever! You can report me to Sir Michael if you want—I don't care. I suppose you must be a friend of his or he wouldn't have let you use this room. But whatever you do, I'm not prepared to hear you say things like that about Becca. You—you didn't know her, and that was your loss, but she wasn't interested in your family for the sort of mercenary motives that you think. There was nothing about the way you lived your lives that attracted her. She wanted Kostas and Nicky and they were enough. But she saw that the—estrangement between you hurt Kostas, so she was hurt too. That's all.'

'A very moving story,' he said cynically. 'Kostas would seem to have chosen a rare gem for his wife. Unfortunately my knowledge of him and his judgment makes that doubtful. However, I give you credit for believing what you say, and for having affection for your sister. But let us not forget that the real issue is Nicos.'

'Nicky isn't an—issue! He's a child, a little human being. He's my nephew as much as yours, and whatever you may think I'm quite capable of bringing him up. And that's what I intend to do,' she added in a little rush.

As she fumbled with the door handle she was afraid that he might come after her and stop her leaving, but he didn't move, and at last she got the door open and shot through it into the outer room under Miss Greystoke's startled gaze.

As she reached the corridor she was crying, and she made straight for the staff cloakroom on the ground floor. Fortunately it was unoccupied, and she sank down on the bench against the wall and let her emotions have their way with her. She was sick and trembling when the tears finally stopped, and the face which stared back at her from the mirror looked pale and ravaged. She bathed her eyes with cool water, and let the tap run over her wrists in an attempt to steady her racing pulses. Then she snatched her blazer from its peg and slung it round her shoulders.

Her thoughts weren't particularly coherent, but the necessity to get Nicky out of London predominated. She had no idea where to go, or how to find a hiding place which Alex Marcos' money would not disclose, but speed was of the essence.

She had a little money in her bag, and more at the flat, and some savings in a building society. If she went to one of the big stations in the rush hour, she thought feverishly, it was unlikely anyone would remember a girl with a young child. She would travel as far as she could afford, and pretend Nicky was hers—that she was an unmarried mother. She could disguise herself, she thought wildly, dye her hair, or buy a wig. If she could lie low for long enough, surely Alex Marcos would get tired of looking for them and return to Greece.

She bit her lip. There was no way she could make that sound convincing to herself. I said I'd fight him, so I'm damned if I'll just give in without a struggle, she thought.

She felt guilty about leaving the company without a word of explanation, or handing in her notice but she had no alternative. She didn't think anyone had seen her leaving the building, but she kept glancing behind her as she anxiously waited for a bus.

Manda looked surprised as she opened the door. 'You're early,' she exclaimed. 'I've just put him down for a nap.'

'Yes,' Harriet forced a smile. 'I'm sorry, Manda, but

I must take him with me. And he won't be coming
tomorrow—or until further notice. In fact I don't know
if—or when. . . .'

Manda gave her a searching look. 'The kettle's just
boiled,' she said. 'Go and make yourself a cup of
something while I get Nicky up and put his coat on. On
your own head be it too,' she added as Harriet moved
obediently towards the kitchen. 'He's hell if he's woken
before he's ready.'

Nicky was plainly disgruntled when he appeared in
Manda's arms, but still too sleepy to be real trouble. He
held his arms out imperatively to Harriet, who took
him, her welcoming smile wavering as she felt his warm
little body curling trustingly into her lap.

'Don't squeeze him to death,' advised Manda,
refilling her own cup. 'What's the matter? Has the
Wicked Uncle appeared and started putting pressure
on?'

Harriet nodded, and Manda sighed. 'Well, I suppose
it was inevitable.' She put out a hand and affectionately
ruffled Nicky's thick dark hair. 'Goodbye, love. Our
yard today—a millionaires' playground tomorrow.
Can't be bad.'

'He's not having him!' Harriet's voice was fierce.

'I admire your spirit, but I don't think you're being
very realistic.' Manda sounded almost matter-of-fact.
'Greeks are very patriarchal, you know, and Nicky has
Marcos blood in his veins. And just suppose you did
persuade his uncle to let you keep him—do you think
Nicky would always be grateful? Unless he was
superhuman, he might start reckoning up on some of
the things he'd missed out on.'

'That's—horrible,' Harriet said slowly.

'Yes, isn't it?' Manda agreed. 'But being an orphan
doesn't automatically confer sanctity as well, you
know.'

'So you think I should just—give him up?' Harriet
was astounded.

'No.' Manda frowned. 'Of course not. But surely you

should be able to do some kind of deal with the Marcos man—agree that Nicky should spend a certain amount of time with you each year.'

Harriet groaned. 'After what's happened today, I don't think he'd agree to Nicky even sending me a Christmas card!' She gave Manda a succinct account of the day's events, and her intentions, and Manda looked startled.

'For heaven's sake, Harriet, don't do anything hasty. If you grab Nicky and start dashing all over the country with him, you'll be giving Alex Marcos the gun to shoot you down with. He may be an arrogant swine, but you won't beat him by acting like a madwoman. You run away and you'll just be playing into his hands.'

'Whose side are you on?' Harriet joked weakly.

'Nicky's.' Manda gave her a gentle smile. 'Take him home if you want, but do some good, hard thinking once you get there. If you don't you could end by losing out completely, and that would be a bad thing for you both.'

Harriet's thoughts were sober as she walked along, pushing the baby buggy. Nicky was fast asleep, his dark lashes making half-moons on his pink cheeks. She looked down at him with tenderness. The thought of losing him was frankly intolerable, but Manda's words had hit home.

At first, as she turned into her road, she was barely aware of the car, and when she did notice it, it was with a kind of detached curiosity. There were plenty of cars in the road, especially at weekends, all the popular models and mostly with elderly registrations, but this was very different.

A Rolls-Royce, she thought incredulously, and her steps began to slow instinctively, her white-knuckled hands gripping the handle of the buggy.

There was a uniformed driver in the front seat, and his passenger was already getting out, tossing his half-smoked cigar into the gutter as he waited for her.

Alex Marcos said with a glittering smile, 'Welcome home, Miss Masters. So this is Nicos. Thank you for bringing him to me.'

CHAPTER TWO

HARRIET stood staring at him. Her lips moved almost helplessly, 'But—I didn't. . . .'

'Oh, I am quite sure you did not,' he said sardonically. 'Nevertheless, the boy is here, and I am here, which is what I wanted.'

Harriet looked down at the sleeping Nicky, and knew that Alex Marcos' gaze had followed her own.

'He is very much a Marcos,' he said after a pause, his voice expressionless.

'He has my sister's eyes.' Harriet's grip tightened almost defeatedly on the handle of the pushchair. She swallowed. 'Will you be taking him now—or do I have time to pack his things?'

'You speak as if I planned to kidnap the child.' He did not bother to disguise the note of irritation in his voice. 'I do not, I promise you. However, this is hardly the place to discuss the matter. Shall we go indoors before we begin to attract unwelcome attention?'

Harriet hesitated, but really she had very little choice, she thought angrily as she began to manoeuvre the pushchair up the rather overgrown path to the front door.

In the hall, she bent to release Nicky. Alex Marcos was at her side.

'Give him to me.' His voice was authoritative, and he took Nicky from her, not waiting for any sign of assent on her part, leaving her to fold the buggy and lead the way up the stairs.

As she unlocked her own door, she was thankful that the room was tidy and clean. She hated coming home at the end of a long day to any kind of mess, and she was glad now that she had made the usual effort to clear up before leaving that morning. She was thankful too that

21

the small clothes-horse only held a selection of Nicky's garments, and none of her own.

'He has not woken,' Alex Marcos said from behind her. 'What shall I do with him?'

Harriet indicated the cot in the corner, shielded from the rest of the room by a small screen which she had recovered herself in a collage of bright pictures cut from magazines.

'He'll sleep for a while,' she said with something of an effort. 'Until he realises it's teatime.'

She watched him put Nicky down in the cot, his movements deft and gentle. Unusually so, she thought, because he could not be a man who was used to children.

He straightened, and turned unsmilingly, the brilliant dark gaze going over the room in candid assessment. Harriet felt an absurd desire to apologise for it. The square of carpet had come from a saleroom, as had much of the furniture. The rest had been picked up from junk shops and lovingly repaired where necessary, and polished, but few of the pieces were beautiful, and none of them were valuable. And besides, there was something in Alex Marcos' sheer physical presence, she realised crossly, that made the surroundings seem far more cramped and shabby than they actually were.

No, she was damned if she would apologise that it was only a room and not a flat, or justify herself in any way. This was her home, and he could make whatever judgments he liked. At the same time, she was his hostess, however reluctant.

She said slowly, 'Can I offer you some refreshment?'—some imp of perversity making her continue, 'I've some sherry left over from Christmas, some instant coffee, or tea-bags.'

He inclined his head mockingly. 'You are most gracious. Perhaps—the coffee.'

She had hoped he would stay where he was, but he followed her along the passage to the first-floor communal kitchen. She could just imagine what he thought of that too, from the elderly gas cooker to the enormous peeling fridge. She opened the cupboard where she kept her provisions and crockery and extracted the coffee and a couple of pottery mugs, while the kettle was boiling.

Alex Marcos was lounging in the doorway, very much at his ease, but not missing a thing, Harriet thought.

She said, 'There's no point in waiting here. The kettle takes rather a long time.'

'I imagine that it might,' he said, smiling faintly.

'It must all be very different from what you're used to,' she said stiffly. 'You should have stayed in the West End, where you belong.'

His brows lifted. 'You have never visited Greece, it is clear, Miss Masters, or you would know that for many of our people such a kitchen would be the height of luxury.'

'But you're not among them.'

'That is true. But my own good fortune does not lead me to feel contempt for the way others lead their lives.'

That wasn't the picture Kostas had painted, Harriet thought, as they went back to the flat. He had spoken with feeling of unyielding pride and arrogance, of a total inability to make allowances for the weakness or feelings of others, or to forgive—and with good reason, considering the way he had been treated by his family. Not his marriage, not Nicky's birth, had done anything to heal whatever breach was between them. Harriet was aware that the Marcos family had been notified when Kostas was killed, but she had frankly never expected to hear from them again. Certainly there had been no flowers, no message of condolence at the funeral. For months there had been silence—and then the bombshell about Nicky had exploded.

Nicky still hadn't stirred when they got back, and Harriet moved round quietly taking his aired clothes from the clothes-horse and folding them, before putting them away in the small chest of drawers. She opened the window a little too, letting some of the later afternoon sunlight into the room, along with the distant noise of traffic, and the overhead throb of a passing jet.

This was the time of day she usually looked forward to—tea with Nicky, then playtime before she got him ready for his bath and bed. But for how many more times? she wondered desolately.

As she turned away from the window, she found Alex Marcos was watching her, and there must have been something about the droop of her shoulders which had betrayed her, because his voice had softened a little as he said, 'You cannot pretend that you wish to spend the rest of your life in this way—looking after someone else's child. You are young. You should be planning a life of your own—children of your own.'

'I'm perfectly content as I am,' Harriet said woodenly.

'You do not wish to marry?' His mouth curled slightly in satirical amusement. 'That is hard to believe. Are you afraid of men?'

Harriet gasped. 'Of course not! How dare you imply. . . .' Her voice tailed away rather helplessly.

He shrugged. 'What else is one to think? You must be aware that you do not lack—attraction.'

His eyes went over her in one swift, sexual assessment which brought the colour roaring into her face.

She didn't know whether to be angrier with him for looking at her like that, or herself for blushing so stupidly. After all, she was reasonably used to being looked over like that. You could hardly work in a large office and avoid it, and Harriet supposed it was part of the 'sexual harassment' that so many women complained of nowadays. But while it remained tacit, and at a distance, she had never felt it was worth complaining about.

But then, she thought furiously, she had never been so frankly or so completely mentally undressed by any man. He had a skin-tingling expertise which rocked her on her heels and made her feel tremblingly vulnerable.

The sound of the kettle's piercing whistle rescued her, and she had to force herself to walk out of the room, not run, with at least a semblance of composure. In the kitchen, she fought for complete control, setting the mugs on a tray and pouring milk into a jug, and sugar into a basin, instead of serving them in their respective containers, as she felt inclined.

It was his constant, unnerving scrutiny which was getting to her, she told herself as she added boiling water to the coffee granules, and not just the sensual element which had intervened. She disliked the knowledge that every detail of her environment, every facet of her life, the way she dressed, moved, spoke and looked, was being continuously judged by a total stranger. If he was looking for faults, he wouldn't have to look far, she thought crossly.

As she carried the tray into the room, he came and took it from her, placing it on a small table in front of the studio couch. He declined both sugar and milk, so her efforts had been a waste of time as she took it black too.

He remained standing, obviously waiting for her to sit down beside him on the studio couch, which made sense as it was the only really comfortable form of seating in the room. She had two high-backed wooden dining chairs tucked back against the wall with her small drop-leaf table, and she wished she had the nerve to go and fetch one of them to establish some kind of independence, but something warned her that he would not interpret her action in that way, and that she might simply be exposing herself to more mocking comments about feminine fears. But she made a point of seating herself as far from him as the width of the couch would permit, and ignored the slightly derisive twist of his lips.

He said silkily, 'Let us return to the subject of Nicos. It is clear that this present situation cannot continue. As he becomes older and more active, these surroundings will become impossible.'

Harriet said coolly, 'I've already been considering

that.' And panicking about it, she thought, but he didn't have to know that.

'And what conclusions have you come to?'

She hedged. 'Well, clearly I'll need a bigger flat—a ground floor one, preferably—with a garden.' Or a castle in Spain, she added silently and hysterically.

Alex Marcos drank some of the coffee. 'You have somewhere in mind, perhaps?' He sounded politely interested, but Harriet was not deceived.

She said with a sigh, 'You know I haven't.'

He nodded. 'And even if such a haven were to present itself, the rent would be beyond your means—is it not so?'

'Yes.' Damn you, she thought. Damn you!

There was a silence. She had begun to shake again inside, and she gulped at the transient comfort the hot coffee gave her, although in terms of Dutch courage she might have done better to opt for the sherry, she thought.

He said at last, 'Miss Masters—if this unhappy business between us were to become a legal battle— what do you imagine a judge would say about the circumstances in which you are trying to raise my nephew?'

Harriet did not meet his gaze. 'I believe—I hope that he would say I was doing my best,' she said wearily.

'I do not doubt that for a moment. But is that what you truly want—a battle in the courts—to make Nicos the subject of gossip and speculation and lurid newspaper stories?'

'I'd have thought you would be used to such things.'

'But I am not the subject under discussion,' he said too softly. 'We are speaking of a two-year-old child, who may one day be embarrassed and emotionally torn by our past battles.'

She gave him an incredulous glance. 'That's blackmail!'

He shrugged. 'I would prefer to describe it as a valid

possibility. He is already old enough to sense conflict and be disturbed by it.'

'And therefore I should just be prepared to hand him over,' Harriet said bitterly. 'I think not, Mr Marcos. Doesn't it occur to you that Nicky might one day wonder why I let him go so easily, and be hurt by it? You're not denying that you intend to separate us permanently?'

'No,' he said. 'That has always been my intention.'

'At least we understand each other,' she said huskily. 'I refuse to let Nicky go under such circumstances.'

'What are you hoping for?' His voice was suddenly harsh. 'A place under my roof for yourself? A more generous financial offer than the one already made? If so, you will be disappointed.'

'I want nothing from you,' Harriet said vehemently. 'The fact that we've even met is your doing, not mine.'

He gave her a weary look. 'Why are you being so stubborn? You are scarcely more than a child yourself. You cannot wish to bear such a burden unaided for perhaps twenty years longer.'

Put like that, it sounded daunting, but Harriet had always faced up to what her responsibilities to Nicky would entail.

'I might ask you the same thing,' she countered. 'All this time you haven't displayed the slightest interest in Nicky. We could both have starved or been homeless for all you knew. Yet now you want him—why?'

'Because it is my duty to care for him,' he said. 'Kostas would have expected it, whatever the relations were between us. The child is of my blood.'

'And mine.'

'Nevertheless,' he said, 'if Kostas had wished you to have charge of the boy, he would have left a document—a will, even a letter saying so. Yet he did not—is it not so?'

Harriet finished her coffee and put the mug down. 'No, there was nothing,' she said after a pause. 'They were so young—too young to be thinking about wills—anything of that kind.'

Alex Marcos' mouth twisted. 'When one has responsibilities Thespinis Masters, one is never too young, and it is never too soon to make provision for the future. Kostas knew, in fact, that if the worst happened, I would take charge of Nicos. He was always happy to shelve his responsibilities.'

Harriet was uneasily aware that her own solicitor had deplored the absence of a will, but she had been too fond of her late brother-in-law to meekly hear him criticised.

'Kostas was too busy being happy and making my sister happy to worry about the worst happening. He was a warm, loving man, so what does it matter if he wasn't perhaps the greatest businessman in the world?'

'If he had stayed with the Marcos Corporation, then it might have mattered a great deal,' Alex Marcos said coldly. 'But we stray towards matters that do not concern you. You will do well to reflect, Miss Masters. At the moment, you claim that Nicky has your whole heart. That is—commendable. But with the money I have offered you, you could buy a new wardrobe—go perhaps for a cruise round the world—meet someone who would make you glad that you are young—and without encumbrances.'

'Gosh, you're insulting!' Harriet muttered between her teeth.

The dark brows rose in exaggerated surprise. 'Why? Because I imply that if you had more time to yourself, you would have little difficulty in attracting a man? I am paying you a compliment.'

'Not as far as I'm concerned. Oddly enough, I quite like my life—and my present *wardrobe*. Marriage isn't the be-all and end-all in my life.'

He smiled. 'So I was right,' he said lazily. 'You are afraid of men.'

'That's ridiculous!'

'What is more,' he said slowly, his eyes never leaving her face, 'you are afraid of me.'

'Nonsense!' said Harriet with a robust conviction she was far from feeling.

His smile widened. His eyes travelled slowly downwards, over the soft swell of her breasts, rising and falling more quickly than she could control under the crisp blouse, then on down to the smooth line of her thighs outlined by the cling of the trim navy skirt, then back, swiftly, to her face where spots of outraged colour were now burning in each cheek.

He said very softly, 'And all this because I—look. What would you do if I touched?'

'Nothing at all,' said Harriet very quickly. 'I'm not afraid, Mr Marcos, just not interested. I expect in your own circle, you find that women are pushovers. Probably a lot of very wealthy men find the same thing. But I don't belong to your circle, I'm not bothered about your money—and frankly, Mr Marcos, you leave me cold.' She paused, aware that her breathing was constricted, and that there was an odd tightening in her throat.

She saw the amusement fade from his eyes, to be replaced by something deeper and more dangerous, saw a muscle jerk in his cheek, and wished desperately that she'd kept quiet. But it was too late to retract or even apologise. He was already reaching for her, his hands not gentle as they pulled her across his hard body.

He said something quietly in his own language, and then he bent his head, putting his mouth on hers with an almost soulless precision.

At first she fought, her lips clamped tight against any deeper invasion, but even then she was aware of other factors subtly undermining her instinctive resistance. Her hands were imprisoned helplessly between their bodies, her palms flat against the wall of his chest, deepening her consciousness of his warm muscularity. The scent of his skin was in her nostrils, emphasised by the faint muskiness of some cologne. If she opened her eyes he would fill her vision, and they seemed enveloped in a cone of silence broken only by their own uneven

breathing. Harriet had been kissed before, but she had
never before known a domination overpowering her
every sense. Ultimately, she had always known she was
in control.

Yet now.... Her lips parted on a little sigh of
capitulation that had nothing to do with coercion
suddenly, because she was as eager as he was, as greedy
for the deeper intimacy he was already seeking, his teeth
grazing the softness of her inner lip, his tongue
delicately and erotically exploring all the soft moist
contours of her mouth.

Gently his hand freed the blouse from her waistband
and his warm fingers moved caressingly on her back
tracing the length of her spine with a featherlight touch
that had her arching against him in unspoken delight.

For the first time in her life, Harriet knew need, knew
the simple and unequivocal ache for fulfilment. And
knew how easy it would be to release the last hold on
sanity and let herself drift inevitably on this warm tide
of pleasure.

And then from the corner, behind the sheltering
screen she heard a small whimpering cry, 'Harry!'

Nicky was awake, and suddenly so was she—jolted
out of her dangerous dream and back in reality.

Alex Marcos had heard the child too. He was no
longer holding her so tightly, and she was able to sit up
and draw away from him, combing shaking fingers
through her fair hair.

Her legs were trembling, but she made herself stand
up, nervously ramming her disordered blouse back into
the waist of her skirt. She stole a sidelong glance at him,
biting her lip.

He was leaning back watching her. His tie was
loosened, and the black hair was dishevelled. His dark
eyes were brilliant, not with thwarted passion, but with
stinging, cynical mockery.

He said softly, 'You were saying something about
your immunity, I think.'

Hot colour flooded her face, and she lifted her hands,

pressing them almost helplessly to her burning cheeks.
Then, as Nicky's whimper threatened to develop into a
wail, she walked across the room and lifted him out of
his cot. Thumb in his mouth, still half asleep, he hitched
a chubby arm round her neck as she carried him
towards the centre of the room. Alex Marcos stood
waiting, hands on hips. Nicky lifted his head and stared
at him.

Harriet said gently, 'This is your uncle Alex, Nicky.
Say hello.'

He wasn't good with strangers. He didn't always
oblige. Perhaps in her secret heart, Harriet hoped this
would be one of those times, and that he would either
become silent and clinging or—which was more likely—
roar with temper.

But he did neither. He summoned a shy engaging
smile and said, ' 'Lo,' before burying his face in
Harriet's shoulder.

Alex spoke to him in Greek, and Harriet felt the little
body in her arms stiffen as if the soft words had
sparked off an association, an elusive memory he was
trying to recapture. Eventually a small muffled voice
said uncertainly, 'Papa?'

Harriet felt tears prick at her eyes.

'Did you have to do that?' she demanded.

'He is half Greek,' Alex said flatly. 'It is right he
should remember and learn to speak his father's
tongue.'

'You heard what he said. He thinks you're his father.'
Harriet spoke fiercely.

'As far as he is concerned, that is what I shall be.
Explanations can wait until he is old enough to
understand.'

'And the succession of surrogate "mothers" in his
life? How old will he be before you explain them?'

He said silkily, 'Guard your tongue, my little English
wasp, or you may have cause to regret it. Yes, I enjoy
the company of women, in bed and out of it. Why
should I deny it? Perhaps you have forgotten that if

Nicos had not woken when he did I might well hav
persuaded you to share some of that—enjoyment.'

Harriet's lips parted in impetuous denial—and close
again in silence.

Alex smiled faintly. 'Very wise,' he approved. 'I hop
you behave with equal wisdom during the rest of ou
dealings together.'

Harriet stared at the floor. She said, 'I would prefe
to deal with Mr Philippides.'

'I'm sure you would,' he said sardonically. 'Now,
wish to get to know my nephew, and preferably withou
your sheltering arms around him. Would it b
convenient for him to spend the weekend with me?'

She glanced up. 'You have a house in London?'

'I have a hotel suite.'

'And you're going to look after him?' Harriet shoo
her head. 'He—he still wears nappies a lot of th
time. . . .'

'I've brought a nursemaid with me from Greece,' h
said impatiently. 'She will deal with such matters, not I.

'I see.' She did see too. She saw his power, and th
certainty and arrogance which that power bestowed
and she hated it. So sure of his ultimate victory tha
he'd even brought a nanny, she thought. 'And if
refuse?'

He lifted his brows. 'Are you sure that you can? You
may resist my claim to total rights, but as his uncle
surely I can demand rights that are equal to yours a
least.' He paused. 'I give you my word I will no
attempt to take the boy out of the country. Will tha
satisfy you?'

Harriet moved her shoulders wearily. 'I doubt if
could stop you, whatever you wanted to do,' she said
'When would you want to collect him? Tomorrow
afternoon? If you give me a time, I'll have his things
ready.'

'Shall we say three o'clock? And I'll return him to
you on Sunday evening.'

'Very well,' she agreed dully. It was the beginning of

the end, she knew. He wouldn't snatch Nicky away as she'd first thought, but detach the child from her by degrees. And there wasn't a thing she could do about it.

He said, 'Until tomorrow, then.' He put out a hand and ruffled Nicky's curls, then ran a finger down his cheek. For a shocked moment, Harriet wondered if he was going to try the same caress on her, because she wasn't at all confident that her reaction would have the necessary cool, but he made no attempt to touch her again.

He said, '*Herete*', and walked out of the room, closing the door behind him.

Harriet stood holding Nicky, her arms tightening round him until he wriggled in protest, demanding to be set down and given his tea. Toast, he wanted, and Marmite and 'ronge'.

'Yes, darling,' she promised penitently, because usually he'd been fed by now at Manda's. But she didn't put him down at once. She carried him over to the window and pulled back the shrouding net curtain, looking into the street below.

Alex Marcos was just about to get into the car. As she watched, he turned and looked up at the window, lifting a hand in mocking acknowledgment of her presence. Furious with herself, Harriet let the curtain fall hurriedly into place, and moved away, wishing that she'd been strong-minded enough to ignore his departure—and wondering why she had failed. . . .

Friday was a miserable day. Harriet had phoned the personnel officer at work first thing and received a sympathetic response when she gave family troubles as the reason for her hasty departure the previous day, and for her continued absence. Then she phoned Manda and told her what had happened, or at least an edited version.

She still found it hard to believe that she had behaved as she did. She had let a man who was almost a stranger, and certainly her enemy, kiss her and arouse feelings within her which had kept her awake and restless most of the night. The warm, airless atmosphere of the room hadn't helped either, and more than once Harriet had found herself wishing wryly for the cliché comfort of a cold shower. But it was only people with money and private bathrooms who could afford such luxuries, she thought regretfully. The bathroom she shared had nothing so sophisticated as a shower in any temperature, and the old-fashioned plumbing made such an infernal din that except in cases of emergency the residents tried to use it as little as possible at night.

Manda heard her explanation of why Nicky would not be spending the day with her without much comment. When Harriet had finished she merely asked, 'And what's he like—Alex Marcos?'

Even in her own ears, Harriet's laugh sounded artificial and she hoped fervently that Manda would assume it was some distortion on the line. 'Oh—just as you'd imagine, I suppose. The answer to the maiden's prayer.'

'Depending, of course,' Manda said gravely, 'on what the maiden happened to be praying for. See you, love. Take care now.'

As she replaced the receiver, Harriet pondered on the real note of warning in Manda's voice, and reflected rather despondently that it was no use trying to fool her, even at a distance.

She tidied and cleaned the flat again almost compulsively, then tucked Nicky into the buggy and took him to the nearby shops which he loved. The sun was shining, and the Italian greengrocer gave him an orange, and Harriet, in a moment of weakness, bought him some sweets. While she was in the newsagents' she treated herself to a daily paper, and some magazines, because she had a whole weekend to fill for once.

Of course she didn't have to stay in the flat, she told herself robustly. She had always promised herself that one day she would do the whole tourist bit—go to the British Museum, or the Zoo, or take a boat down to

Greenwich—but she had always put the idea to the back of her mind, telling herself it could wait till Nicky was older and could enjoy it with her. Well, there seemed little point in delaying any longer, she thought, with a kind of unhappy resolution.

She cooked Nicky's favourite food for lunch—fish fingers, baked beans and oven chips. Manda, who believed in wholefoods and a balanced diet, would have frowned a little, but Nicky was jubilant and ate every scrap, including the ice cream which followed.

Harriet tried to explain to him that he was going to have a little holiday with his uncle, but wasn't sure how much she'd got through to him, because he seemed far more interested in his toy cars than in the fact that she was packing his night things and the best of his clothes in a small case.

He's only a baby, she thought as she watched him play, quite oblivious to her own mental and emotional turmoil. He's too little to be taken from all the security he knows, and be made to speak Greek, and all the other things he'll have to learn.

Yet on the other hand there was the very real danger that out of love and inexperience she might keep him a baby too long, might try too hard to protect him from the world which he was as much a part of as she was herself. A man's influence in his life was probably essential, Harriet thought—but what would be the effect of someone like Alex Marcos, wealthy, cynical and amoral, on the mind of an impressionable child?

It was inevitable that when she sat down with the newspaper and a cup of coffee while Nicky played on the carpet at her feet, Alex's picture should be the first to leap out at her. And, again, inevitably, it was the gossip column, and he wasn't alone. He was sitting at a table in a restaurant or a night club—Harriet didn't recognise the name anyway—and the girl beside him, smiling radiantly at the camera, had her arm through his and her head on his shoulder.

Her red head on his shoulder, Harriet discovered as

she read through the piece that accompanied the photograph. Alex, it said, was in London on business and lovely model Vicky Hanlon was just the girl to help him unwind from his busy schedule.

After an unctuous dwelling on Vicky Hanlon's physical attributes which would have had even the mildest Women's Libber spitting carpet tacks and reaching for the telephone, the columnist quoted her as saying, 'Poor Alex leads such a hectic life. I just want to help him relax as much as possible.'

'Yuck!' said Harriet violently, dropping the paper as if it had bitten her. She marched down the passage to the bathroom and washed her face and cleaned her teeth thoroughly which, while a relatively futile gesture, nevertheless made her feel better.

She was increasingly on edge as three o'clock approached. Nicky had grown tired of his toys and demanded a story, and she was just following The Little Gingerbread Man with the Three Billy Goats Gruff when she heard the sound of a car door slam in the street below.

Her voice hesitated and died away right in the middle of the troll's threat, and her whole body tensed. Nicky bounced plaintively and said, 'Troll.'

She hugged him fiercely. 'Another time, darling. Your—your uncle's come to fetch you, and you're going to have a wonderful time.'

She remembered what Alex had said the previous day about her sheltering arms and was careful to let Nicky walk beside her to the door as the buzzer sounded imperatively.

Her palms were damp, and her mouth was dry. She had brushed her hair until it shone, and the dress she was wearing, although simple and sleeveless, was the most becoming in her wardrobe, its cool blues and greens accentuating her fairness, and the very fact that she had chosen to wear it was evidence enough that she was on the verge of making a complete and utter fool of herself.

She made herself reach out and release the Yale knob and turn the handle.

There was a man outside, stockily built and swarthy in a chauffeur's uniform, his cap under one arm, and accompanied by a middle-aged woman with greying black hair who looked nervous.

It was the woman who spoke. 'Thespinis Masters—I am Yannina. I have come from Kyrios Marcos to fetch his nephew, the little Nicos.' Her anxious expression splintered into a broad smile as she spied Nicky, who had relapsed into instant shyness at the sight of strangers and who was peering at them from behind Harriet's skirt.

She crouched down, holding out her arms and murmuring encouragingly in Greek, and slowly Nicky edged towards her.

Harriet picked up his case and handed it to the chauffeur, who nodded respectfully to her.

'Kyrios Marcos wishes to assure you that the boy will be returned to you on Sunday evening, not later than six o'clock,' he said in careful heavily accented English.

'Thank you.' Harriet hesitated. 'I—I thought he would be coming to fetch Nicky himself.'

The chauffeur looked surprised. 'He is waiting below in the car, *thespinis*. If you have a message for him, I would be glad to convey it.'

Not, Harriet thought, the sort of message I have in mind. She forced a smile and shook her head, and stepped backward as Yannina took Nicky's hand and began to lead him away. He looked back once and grinned and waved, and Harriet felt a lump rise in her throat as she shut the door between them.

This time, wild horses weren't going to drag her to the window to watch them go.

So he'd decided to stay downstairs in the car, which was a delicate way of telling her not to read too much into a kiss. Had he sensed something in her untutored, unguarded response to what he would regard as quite a casual caress that had warned him it might be kinder to keep his distance?

The thought shamed her to the core. She felt sick and empty, and although she tried to blame this on Nicky's carefree departure, she knew she was fooling herself.

The unpalatable truth she had to face was that every nerve, every pulse beat in her body had been counting away the hours, the minutes, the seconds before she saw Alex Marcos again. She knew too that the ache beginning inside her now was deeper and more wounding than mere disappointment or injured pride, and she remembered Manda's warning, and was frightened.

CHAPTER THREE

Harriet felt pleasantly tired as she walked back towards the house late on Saturday evening. She had done all the things she had promised herself to do, and had managed to fill her day too full for thought, even treating herself to the pure luxury of afternoon tea at a hotel.

When Becca had been carrying Nicky, she had once laughingly remarked that when you were pregnant, every second person you met seemed to be in the same condition. Paradoxically, Harriet thought, when you were alone, everyone else seemed to be in couples. But then London had always been a bad place in which to be solitary.

But she didn't have to be alone, she told herself. If and when Nicky went to Greece, she would find a flat to share with girls of her own age. There were plenty advertised.

She opened the front door and walked into the hall, to be pounced on by one of the downstairs tenants, looking severe. 'Three times!' she announced with a kind of annoyed triumph. 'That's how many times the phone has rung for you in the past hour and a half, Miss Masters, and you not here!'

'I'm sorry,' said Harriet in bewilderment. 'Was there a message?'

Mrs Robertson produced a slip of paper. 'You're to ring this number and ask for this extension. And now if I might get back to my television programme,' she added aggressively as if she suspected Harriet of being in league with the unknown caller to keep her from the last few minutes of 'Dynasty'.

Harriet dialled, and was answered from the switchboard of a famous London hotel. Faintly she gave the

extension number, thinking frantically, 'Nicky—oh no
something's happened to Nicky!'

Alex Marcos answered so promptly that he might
have been waiting by the phone. Her heart gave the
oddest bound when she heard his voice, and then she
was aware of something else—background noises which
were quite unmistakably Nicky screaming with temper.

She asked in swift alarm, 'Is he ill?'

'His health is perfect,' Alex Marcos said grimly. 'I
wish I could say the same for his disposition. He seems
to have been thoroughly spoilt. Last night, Yannina
managed to get him to sleep with difficulty. This
evening it has been quite impossible. Everything she has
tried with him has failed. He merely screams all the
louder and cries for you.'

'He's not at all spoilt,' Harriet said indignantly. 'I
really don't know what else you expected. He's far too
young to take such a complete change in his
environment in his stride. He's in a strange room with
strange faces round him, and he's frightened.'

'You have missed your vocation, Miss Masters. You
should clearly have been a child psychologist,' he
drawled. 'Did it occur to you to warn Yannina that he
might react in this way?'

Harriet sighed. 'I honestly didn't know. He—he went
with her willingly enough. And I tried to explain that it
was a little holiday. . . .'

He said tightly, 'Very well, Miss Masters, you are
absolved. He is, as you say, a very young child, and he
is deeply distressed. If I send my car for you, will you
come to him?'

Harriet swallowed. 'Of course.'

She heard his phone go down, and replaced her own
receiver.

She went upstairs to the flat and stood looking round
rather helplessly, wondering what she should do. She
didn't know whether or not she should pack a bag with
some overnight essentials. Nothing had been said about
her staying the night with Nicky, and perhaps she

would just be expected to get him calm and off to sleep before she was chauffeured back here again.

In the end, she compromised by tucking some clean undies and her toothbrush into the bottom of her biggest shoulder bag.

The car was at the door almost before it seemed possible. She would have preferred to sit in the front with the driver, but she was gravely ushered into the back, and even offered a rug to put round her, which she declined.

It had all happened so fast that she hadn't time to be nervous or consider the implications of what she was doing, or not until now. Sitting alone in the car's unaccustomed luxury, she tried to compose her thoughts and emotions, reminding herself over and over again that she was only seeing Alex Marcos again because Nicky needed her, and that her concern must be for him.

She even began to wonder whether Alex might be having second thoughts about taking Nicky to Greece, with the prospect of nightly scenes to contend with.

The suite Alex occupied was on the second floor of the hotel, and as soon as Harriet left the lift, she could hear Nicky roaring.

The chauffeur led her along the corridor and knocked deferentially. Alex opened the door himself. He was casually dressed in close-fitting dark slacks and a loose sweatshirt, and in spite of his ill-temper, he looked more attractive than ever, Harriet thought, her stomach tying itself in knots.

She said insanely, 'We should have called him Macbeth!'

He stared at her. 'What in heaven's name are you talking about?'

'It's the play,' she said quickly. 'By Shakespeare. Macbeth murdered sleep in it, when he murdered Duncan.'

His mouth twisted. 'I imagine my unfortunate neighbours in the adjoining suites may well be contemplating the same solution. There have already been discreet enquiries from the management, you understand.' He shook her head. 'I never knew a child's lungs could have such power!'

There was a cot in Nicky's room and he was standing up in it, gripping the bars with small desperate fists, his face swollen and blubbered with weeping. Yannina sat on a chair facing him, her motherly face contorted with a kind of despair as she talked to him in a swift monotone. A congealing cup of milk on a side table, and various untouched fruit drinks, bore mute witness to her attempts to find some form of pacification. As she entered the room, Harriet's foot turned against something soft and she looked down to see Nicky's teddy bear. She bent and retrieved it. Hurling his beloved toy across the room was the ultimate in despairing gestures as far as Nicky was concerned.

He was quiet as Harriet approached the cot, his whole being indrawn, intent on producing the next explosion of anguish at the maximum volume. And then he saw her. He screamed again, but on a different note, and his arms reached for her imperatively.

As she lifted him, he clutched at her fiercely, clinging like a damp limpet.

'Thespinis Masters, I am sorry, so sorry.' Yannina was almost weeping herself. 'He wanted nothing and no one only you.'

Harriet gave her a reassuring smile and began walking up and down the room with Nicky, holding him tightly and crooning wordlessly to him, as Becca had done when he was teething. Slowly the convulsive sobs tearing at his body began to weaken until he was quiet, except for the occasional hiccup. Gradually one hand relinquished its painful hold on her neck, and she knew instinctively that his thumb had gone to his mouth. His weight had altered too. He seemed heavier because he had relaxed, and Harriet knew that he was probably more than half asleep.

Confirming this, Yannina whispered 'His eyes are

closing. *Thespinis*, may God be praised! Ah, the poor
little one!' She moved to the cot and began
straightening and smoothing the sheets and blankets
and shaking up the single pillow.

Harriet turned and began another length of the room,
slowing her pace deliberately. As she did so, she saw Alex
standing in the doorway watching her, his brows drawn
together in a thunderous frown. She bit her lip. Clearly
her methods with Nicky did not have his approval, so why
then had he sent for her? She ventured another glance at
the doorway and saw that he had gone.

When she was sure that Nicky had slipped over the
edge of drowsiness into actual slumber, she carried him
to the cot and placed him gently in it, smoothing the
covers with care over his small body. His face was still
blotched with tears, she saw with a pang. She
straightened with a sigh, and went to the door where
Yannina was waiting for her, looking round first to
make sure that Nicky hadn't stirred.

She had been too eager to get to his side to take much
notice of her surroundings previously, but now she
realised that she was in a large sitting room, off which
the other rooms presumably opened.

A waiter had appeared with a trolley, and Harriet
saw to her astonishment that covers were being
whipped deftly off an assortment of delicious-looking
sandwiches and other savouries, and that there was a
bottle of champagne cooling on ice.

Alex was lounging on one of the thickly cushioned
sofas, but he rose as she came rather uncertainly into
the room. He had stopped frowning, she saw, but the
rather formal smile he gave her did not reach his eyes.

'Champagne is the best pick-me-up in the world,' he
said. 'I am sure you are as much in need of it as I am.'

Harriet thought wryly of the other two occasions in
her life when she had drunk champagne—at Becca's
wedding, and Nicky's christening. She had always
regarded it as a form of luxurious celebration rather
than a tonic, but she was willing to be convinced.

She chose a seat on the sofa facing the one which Alex was occupying, and pretended she did not see the expression of derision which flitted across his face.

He tipped the waiter and dismissed him with a nod.

'Please help yourself,' he told Harriet courteously. 'I hope you like smoked salmon.'

Harriet murmured something evasive. She was damned if she was going to admit she hadn't the faintest idea whether she liked it or not. And that bowl full of something black and glistening—surely that couldn't be caviare? There were vol-au-vents too, filled with chicken and mushroom in a creamy sauce. It was all a far cry from the scrambled eggs on toast she had planned for supper. And she was hungry too. Her tea seemed a very long time ago, but at the same time she knew that Alex's presence would have an inhibiting effect on her appetite.

She took the tall slender glass he unsmilingly handed her, and sipped some of the wine it contained, wishing for the first time in her life that she knew enough about wines to appreciate the vintage.

She tasted a little of everything on the trolley, aware all the time of the sombre scrutiny of the man who sat opposite. He ate nothing, she noticed, merely drinking his wine and refilling the glasses when it became necessary.

Alex broke the silence at last. 'I tried several times to telephone you this evening.' His brow lifted sardonically. 'I began to wonder if you had taken advantage of Nicky's absence to spend the night with your lover.'

Aware that she was being baited, Harriet smiled sweetly and confined her reply to, 'No.'

'Nevertheless my summons to you must have upset your plans in some way at least.'

Harriet thought without regret of the scrambled eggs. 'Only slightly.'

'You are fortunate. I had to postpone an appointment this evening.'

Another relaxation session with his beautiful redhead? Harriet wondered.

It was probably the champagne which made her say, 'Never mind, Mr Marcos. I'm sure she'll forgive you.'

A faint smile touched the corners of his mouth. 'Now what makes you think my appointment was with a woman? You should not believe everything you read in the papers.'

'I don't,' she denied with more haste than dignity. 'Read the papers, I mean—or at least read about you in them.'

'You surprise me. Judging by some of your remarks to Philippides, I imagined you had made a lifelong study of my way of life through their columns.' Narrowing his eyes, he held up his glass, studying with apparent fascination the bubbles rising to its rim.

'Eavesdroppers,' Harriet said sedately, taking another smoked salmon sandwich, 'rarely hear any good of themselves. How did you know my telephone number anyway?'

He sighed. 'I made a note of it as I was leaving yesterday—in case of just such an emergency as this.'

'Well, I hardly imagined it would be for any other reason,' Harriet snapped.

'Have some more champagne.' He refilled her glass. 'Perhaps it will sweeten your disposition.'

'I don't think so,' she said. 'Nicky gets his temper from my side of the family.'

'You alarm me. The Marcos temper is also supposed to be formidable.'

'Poor Nicky. He may never smile again,' Harriet said cheerfully.

'That is what I am afraid of,' he murmured. 'Will he sleep now until morning, do you suppose?'

'I think he will.' She looked round for her bag. 'I—I really ought to be going.'

'I think not,' said Alex. 'In my opinion it would be far better if you were here when the child awakes.'

Harriet didn't meet his gaze. 'You mean—you'd like me to come back first thing in the morning.'

'I mean nothing of the kind,' he said irritably. 'I am suggesting that you stay the night here.'

Harriet continued to stare at the carpet. 'I really think it would be better if I went home.'

'And I cannot formulate one good reason why you should do so.' The dark eyes glittered wickedly. 'Why so reluctant, Harriet *mou*? Are you perhaps afraid that the bed I'm offering you is my own?'

She decided prudently that she had had enough champagne and put the glass down.

She said, 'No, I'm not, but I admit that remarks like that aren't very reassuring.'

His mouth twisted. 'Is that what you want—reassurance?'

She said wearily, 'I don't want anything from you, Mr Marcos. I came here tonight because Nicky needs me, not to indulge in verbal or any other kind of battles with you. I think I'd better go home.'

'No, stay,' he said, and there was the authentic note of the autocrat in his voice. 'I admit it amuses me to make you blush, but I have no designs on your virtue. And if I was in the mood for a woman tonight, I would choose a willing partner, and not a frightened virgin,' he added, the dark eyes flicking cruelly over her.

Harriet hadn't the slightest wish to afford him any more amusement, but she could do nothing to prevent the betraying colour rising in her face. He made being a virgin sound like an insult, she thought fiercely, and knew a momentary impulse to categorically deny she was any such thing which she hastily subdued. He was in a strange mood tonight, and she already knew to her cost how unpredictable he could be.

Trying to sound composed, she said, 'Thank you. Do I share Nicky's room? I saw there was a bed in there and. . . .'

'No,' he said. 'Yannina sleeps there. Your room is

there.' He nodded at a door on the opposite side of the room.

Harriet was taken aback. 'But if Nicky wakes up. . . .' she began.

'Then Yannina will no doubt call you,' he said impatiently. 'Why make difficulties where there are none? Everything has been prepared for you in there.'

Harriet suppressed a sigh. 'Very well. Goodnight, Mr Marcos.'

He gave her a sardonic look. 'As we shall be sharing a bathroom, perhaps you had better call me Alex.' He laughed at her startled expression. 'Don't look so stricken,' he mocked. 'There is a bolt on the inside of the door which you may use. Do you make all this fuss at your house where every day you share a bathroom with half a dozen other people or more?'

That, Harriet thought, was a different matter entirely, and he knew it.

She said calmly, 'My only concern, Mr Marcos, is that I seem to be putting you to a great deal of inconvenience.'

'I am becoming accustomed to that.' As Harriet rose to her feet, he got up too. 'And I told you to call me Alex.'

'I see no need for that,' Harriet said quietly. 'After all, we—we are strangers—or comparatively so,' she added as she began to laugh again.

'Strangers?' he queried. 'You have a short memory, little one. Adversaries, perhaps, but hardly strangers.' For a moment the dark eyes rested almost speculatively on her mouth, and Harriet felt herself quiver inwardly.

'Yes, well,' she said idiotically, 'I think I'll go to bed.'

He grinned and moved forward, and Harriet made herself stand her ground. She was thankful she had done so, and not jumped away like a fool, because he was only reaching for more champagne, and not for her at all.

She gave him a meaningless smile and walked across to the door he had indicated, aware that he was

watching her every step of the way. It was a relief to
close the door between them.

It was a large room, luxuriously and efficiently
furnished in shades of beige and chocolate, but
anonymous just the same in the way that so many hotel
rooms are. The bathroom wasn't much smaller, with a
shower cubicle and a sunken bath hidden behind smoked
glass doors, and basins sunk in a vanitory unit which
ran the length of one wall, with mirrors above lit like a
film star's dressing room. There was an abundance of
towels, and in one of the cupboards of the unit, Harriet
found tissues, shampoos, heated rollers and a hair-dryer.

She caught a glimpse of herself in one of the mirrors
as she straightened, and bit her lip. She wasn't just slim,
she was thin, and her face looked pale and strained. Her
navy shirtwaister was clean and reasonably becoming,
but it wouldn't knock anyone's eye out either.

There was a towelling bathrobe hanging on the door
which presumably led to Alex's room, and a leather
toilet case spilling its contents across one of the surfaces
of the unit. There was a faint scent of cologne in the air
which Harriet recognised instantly, as it assaulted her
nostrils with an unbearable familiarity.

One kiss, she told herself with a kind of despair.
That's all it was. No big deal, and certainly nothing to
build the rest of your life around.

But for the first time she wished she was someone
entirely different, someone wordly and experienced,
who regarded sex as one of the many pleasures life had
to bestow. Someone who would attract Alex Marcos,
and who could signal without words that she was the
kind of willing partner he desired.

But that's not me, she told herself forlornly. All I
ever signal are my hang-ups.

As she went back into the bedroom, she suddenly
found she was thinking of Kostas and Becca. It was
incredible that Alex and Kostas were actually brothers.
Apart from a passing physical likeness, there was hardly
a point of resemblance between them.

Harriet remembered wistfully how much in love they had been. How strong Kostas had always been with her sister, how tender and protective. And when Nicky had been born, he had been hardly able to contain his pride in them both.

It was impossible to imagine Alex in similar circumstances. The role of besotted husband and father would sit oddly on his cynical shoulders. He took women, used them and let them go. She could remember Kostas saying so with a rueful shrug.

'I pity his wife, when he marries,' he had said. 'But no doubt Mama will find him a discreet Greek girl who will pretend not to mind that he is not faithful to her.'

'I'd mind,' Harriet thought violently. 'If he so much as looked at another woman, I'd mind like hell.' She paused, horrified at the tenor of her own thoughts.

She sat down on the edge of one of the beds, lacing her fingers tightly together in her lap. All this could so easily have been avoided, she thought. If only she hadn't lost her temper and sounded off to Mr Philippides, she might never have met Alex, or at least if she had it would simply have been for very formal discussions in lawyers' offices. Never alone, she thought painfully.

She gave herself a mental shake. She was depressed because she was tired after wandering round London all day long, and then the unexpected nervous hassle of coping with Nicky. And she wasn't used to champagne. That was why her thoughts were flying wildly in all sorts of unexpected and unwanted directions. Sleep, she decided, was what she needed.

She was momentarily diverted by finding a vast tentlike nightgown folded on the other bed. It was made of white cotton with insertions of lace, like something from another century, and had a high neck and long sleeves. For a moment, Harriet thought furiously it was a malicious gesture from Alex, and then she realised shamedly that it must belong to Yannina, whose well-meaning kindness was beyond reproach.

She wasn't sure whether she could cope with being swathed in so many yards of material in bed, but as a dressing gown, it would be superb. She undressed and put it on, smiling at the voluminous ripples of white falling round her bare feet. And then she remembered that she had left her bag with her toothbrush in it on the sofa in the sitting room. For a moment she contemplated getting dressed again, then she went over to the bedroom door and opened it a cautious crack.

The trolley and the champagne bucket had disappeared, and the room was empty, lit only by one lamp burning in the corner. There were no lights showing under any doors but her own, and Harriet guessed that Alex had gone off to keep his appointment, albeit belatedly.

She gathered up the folds of nightdress so that she wouldn't trip, and walked across to the sofa. As she picked up her bag, she heard the sound of a key in the main door of the suite, and turned frantically to run for cover. But even as she did so an escaping fold of nightgown caught on a small occasional table standing by the sofa and overturned it, together with the ashtray it supported.

Harriet muttered, 'Oh, no!' and knelt resignedly to retrieve it. As she did so, she heard the door open and close and Alex's voice say, 'Holy Saints!'

She straightened slowly, and turned to face him. She was prepared for amusement, but he wasn't laughing. There was an odd, arrested startled look on his face which slowly gave way to a kind of anger, but he certainly wasn't laughing.

'I'm sorry.' For no reason she could fathom, Harriet felt she had to apologise. She held up her bag. 'I—I was looking for a toothbrush.'

He said nothing. His swift, impatient stride took him past her, through her room and into the bathroom beyond. As Harriet trailed awkwardly after him, he opened a cupboard and produced a handful of new toothbrushes in cellophane wrappers which he tossed on to the unit.

He looked at her with a kind of weary resignation, 'Is there anything else you need—Miss Masters?'

She said huskily, 'No—yes, I mean—could you show me how the shower operates?'

'It would be a pleasure,' he said with icy formality.

The floor tiles felt cold under her bare feet as she stood and watched him demonstrate the various dials and levers. At last he switched on the water and adjusted the temperature.

'Are you going to use this thing?' he asked. 'Or would you find the bath easier?'

'The shower will be fine,' she said hastily. 'Thank you very much.' She put her bag down on the vanitory unit and waited for him to go.

He stood watching her, his dark eyes cool and speculative. She was totally covered from throat to feet—Yannina's nightdress was probably the most totally opaque garment in the history of the world—but she felt as if she was naked. Her throat began to close up nervously.

Alex said softly, 'Why do you not take your shower? Do you need more help?'

She wasn't capable of moving. She stood quite still as he walked towards her. Almost detachedly he reached out a hand and began to undo the long row of buttons down the front of the nightdress. There seemed to be no sound in the room other than the gentle splash of water on to the tiles in the shower cubicle, and her own ragged, tortuous breathing.

When he had unfastened the last button, Alex's hand moved back to the prim neckline, pushing aside the lace-trimmed collar as his fingers found the silky skin beneath in a caress as soft as the brush of a butterfly's wing. He stroked her throat, lingering momentarily on the convulsive leap of the pulse at its base, then moved his hand smoothly and gently along the supple line of her bare shoulder, easing the nightgown away from her body as he did so.

He said smoothly and cynically, 'Before I am carried away by the vision of your naked loveliness, my English rose, may I know from your own lips that this is what you want?'

Harriet stared at him, her eyes widening in shocked incredulity as he went on, 'It occurs to me that this is some ploy of yours to retain control of Nicos—either by taking me to the point of no return, and then coyly refusing, or by seeking to appeal to my generosity by the sweetness of your surrender.' He smiled coldly down into her paling face. 'I should warn you now, Harriet *mou*, that neither tactic will work. Besides, a girl's first time with a man is rarely comfortable or particularly rewarding, and I would hate to think you were making such a sacrifice for all the wrong reasons.'

She said in a choking voice, 'You're—vile!'

'Ah!' He grinned mockingly and stepped back, away from her. 'Do I take it that you have changed your mind about giving yourself to me?'

Harriet felt sick. 'I——I never intended. . . .'

'No?' Alex lifted his brows disbelievingly. 'Then it was all a coincidence that you just happened to be in the other room when I returned—that you happened to need a toothbrush—that you happened to want a shower? And this travesty of a garment with its frills and little buttons—was that too part of the plan? If so, my congratulations. Removing it would have been a great and lingering pleasure.'

'The nightdress belongs to Yannina—as you're probably well aware.' Harriet dragged the gaping edges at her throat together with a hand that shook. 'And none of your rotten insinuations are true. I'm here because you needed help with Nicky—not because I wanted to be. I never wanted to see you again—and as for lying in wait, hoping for an opportunity to—to seduce you—good grief, that's the last thing I wanted!' She paused for breath. 'And as for the shower,' she added savagely, 'strange as it may seem to a—a conceited, arrogant—ape like you, I've never had one

before. I didn't know how it worked—and I didn't want
to be frozen or scalded. . . .'

'Then try it now,' he said between his teeth, his
face dark with temper. 'You should find it exactly
right.'

He picked her up, kicking and struggling, and
dumped her, nightdress and all, directly under the full
jet of water. Drenched and gasping, she slipped on the
wet tiles and sat down heavily, trapped in the clinging
yards of material, hearing dimly above the noise of the
water the slam of the bathroom door as he left.

Somehow she managed to reduce the flow, and then
switch it off completely. Shivering with rage, she
stripped off the soaking nightdress and hurled it, a
dripping bundle, into the corner, before snatching one
of the voluminous bath sheets provided by the hotel
and wrapping herself in it. She stormed back into her
room and kicked the door shut behind her. She was a
sorry sight, innumerable little rivulets from her wet hair
running down her back and shoulders. Ruefully she
dabbed her face dry, and wrung as much water from the
ends of her hair as she could, before rubbing it
vigorously with an end of the towel.

She was still shaking inside, and she felt close to
tears. She tried to tell herself that Alex's cynical
misinterpretation of her motives and behaviour was all
to the good. For those few moments, just his lightest
touch on her skin had had her dizzy with wanting him.
Right now, she might have been in bed with him, and
that would have been disastrous, because the last thing
she wanted was to be just another in a long line of
women. And what she did want from Alex was
something she didn't even dare to contemplate.

She wanted to fetch the hair-dryer she had noticed
earlier, but she didn't dare. Alex might hear her moving
about, opening cupboards, and she couldn't face
another confrontation.

In fact, if it hadn't been for Nicky waking the next
morning and perhaps calling out for her, she would

have dressed and gone home, even if she had to walk all the way.

She draped the bath sheet over the long radiator under the central window and crept into bed. It was a warm night, but it was a long time before she stopped shivering, and an hour after that before her chaotically whirling thoughts began to blur at the edges, and she slipped gradually into a restless sleep haunted by strange and disturbing images.

She dreamed she was alone, and that she was crying because she was alone, and there was no comfort anywhere. And then suddenly there were arms around her which were warm and strong, and held her closely, and she dreamed she turned to that strength, like a flower to the sun, whispering, 'Alex,' and smiling in her sleep.

CHAPTER FOUR

THE dream seemed so real that it was almost a shock when she opened reluctant eyes the next morning and found she was alone. She sat up slowly, pushing her hair back from her face, and wondering what had woken her, and then she heard the soft knock on the door and Yannina's voice, 'Thespinis Masters—the little one has woken and is asking for you.'

'I'll be there right away,' Harriet called, pushing back the bedclothes. She put on the clean undies she had brought with her and washed swiftly, a wary eye on the door which led to Alex's room, but there was no sound at all.

As soon as she was dressed, she went straight to Nicky's room. A small table and chair had been installed, and he was sitting there in his pyjamas, watery-eyed but silent, dividing looks of acute suspicion between Yannina and the bowl of his favourite milky cereal before him.

'Good morning, scamp.' Harriet ruffled his hair teasing. 'Is breakfast no longer being eaten in these circles?'

Nicky's smile wavering at first lit up his whole face enchantingly. He picked up his spoon and began to eat with his usual gargantuan appetite, occasionally stealing glances at Harriet to make sure she had not gone away.

Yannina sighed. 'It is you that he needs, *thespinis*,' she said rather sadly. 'It was a blessing you were able to come to him so swiftly. I hope you slept in God's good health.'

'Yes.' Harriet hesitated. 'Yannina—I'm afraid I had a slight accident last night. I was trying to find how the shower worked, and it—it came on rather unexpectedly and your lovely nightdress got very wet.'

55

'*Po, po, po,*' Yannina shrugged, her rather anxious face softening warmly. 'It is nothing, *thespinis*. You are welcome to anything I have. A little water matters not at all. You must not concern yourself.'

She clearly thought the faint flush that had risen in Harriet's cheeks had been put there by guilt and remorse over the fate of the nightdress, and Harriet could only devoutly be thankful the good woman had no idea of the truth.

She lingered as long as possible, watching Nicky eat the rest of his breakfast, and then getting washed and dressed in his favourite tee-shirt and shorts. Yannina was already clearly his slave and he knew it, which wasn't altogether a good thing, thought Harriet wryly, but there was nothing she could say or do. Soon Nicky's character building and training would be out of her hands completely.

When Yannina had asked her for the third time with increasing astonishment if she herself was not hungry for her own breakfast, she realised that she could not hang round Nicky's room like a spare part all morning.

She had to nerve herself to go back in the sitting room. Alex was sitting at a table which had been set in the window, deep in the financial pages of one of the Sunday papers. He rose politely as Harriet hesitated, and indicated that she should join him, his face unsmiling and enigmatic. He was wearing a dark suit this morning, she noticed. The jacket was tossed across a nearby chair, and he was tieless, with both his waistcoat and several buttons on his immaculate shirt left casually undone, so that the strong brown column of his throat and the beginnings of the curling mat of dark hair on his chest were visible.

She sat down, not looking at him, concentrating on shaking out the linen napkin and spreading it across her lap.

'Orange juice?' Alex asked. 'Croissants? Or would you prefer eggs and bacon?'

She shook her head, murmuring a faint negative,

because it seemed unlikely she would be able to force a crumb past her lips anyway. The orange juice was easy enough, freshly squeezed, slightly tart and totally delicious, and that, combined with the sun coming warmly and benignly through the window, made her spirits begin to rise a little.

A waiter appeared as if by magic with a pot of fresh coffee, and a basket crammed with rolls, still hot to the touch, and flaky croissants. The smell of warm, fresh bread was irresistible and Harriet succumbed, although she was still on edge, waiting for Alex to say something—anything. Fresh bread and tension, she thought ruefully. I shall probably die of indigestion.

He was being very civil, pouring her coffee and passing her butter and cherry jam almost before she was aware she wanted them, but apart from that his attention seemed wholly absorbed in his newspaper.

At last, when he folded it and put it aside, she decided she had better break the silence.

She said rather nervously, 'I'm sure Nicky will be fine now. I really ought to go home.'

'I wish I shared your optimism.' He gave her a long look. 'Did it take a long time for Nicos to adjust to you after my brother and his wife were killed?'

She hesitated. 'He was disturbed, naturally, but I—I'd always been there. I actually lived with them, so he was used to me. He used to ask for them both constantly, of course. He still does.'

'And what do you say?'

She shrugged. 'I'm afraid I evade the issue—distract him with something. I'm not a psychologist and I don't know how to handle it. He's too young to understand the truth.'

He nodded expressionlessly, and made no further comment, merely asking if she wanted more coffee.

'No, thanks.' Harriet put her crumpled napkin on the table. 'I really should be getting back.'

'Why?' he asked. 'You have some urgent appointment, perhaps?'

'Of course not. It's Sunday.'

'And what do you usually do on Sundays?' He drank the last of his coffee, watching her over the rim of the cup.

She shrugged. 'Tidy the flat—make lunch—take Nicky to a park if it's fine.'

'It sounds a reasonable plan,' he said. 'And it can be as easily carried out here as at your dismal room.'

'No,' said Harriet. Her hands were beginning to tremble again, and she wedged them together in her lap below the edge of the table. 'I—I do have a life of my own to lead, and I have things to do.'

He gave her a derisive look. 'You made me believe that Nicos was your whole life. Is it not so?'

'And you've made me believe that it's time I thought differently,' she said flatly. 'So that's what I'm going to do, starting now.'

'I wish it could be as simple as that. It must be obvious from Nicos' reaction last night, and to a lesser extent on the previous evening, that he will need a substantial—period of adjustment to his new circumstances.' He paused. 'I am going to need your help— Miss Masters.'

Harriet ignored the unmistakable note of mockery investing the last two words. 'My help? I thought you couldn't wait to remove Nicky from my sphere of influence altogether.'

'But then I was not aware of the extent of his dependence on you,' he said coldly. 'You have made yourself necessary to the child.'

'Oh, I'm so sorry,' said Harriet with immense sarcasm. 'Of course I see now I should have neglected and ill-treated him, just to make things easier for you. What a pity I didn't realise earlier that you were going to come marching into our lives like—like. . . .'

'Like a tyrant,' he supplied too softly. 'Or—a conceited, arrogant ape.'

'Yes,' she said defiantly. 'Exactly like that.'

'I wonder,' he said after another, longer pause,

'why no one has ever beaten you soundly, Harriet *mou.*'

She had never felt less like smiling, but in spite of herself the corners of her mouth turned up wryly. She said, 'Probably because I seem to—to get along with most people.'

'And I think, for Nicos' sake, you are going to have to make an effort to get along with me. Can we at least agree that his wellbeing is of paramount importance?'

'Yes,' she acknowledged dully. She knew what was coming—another reasoned argument why Nicky would be so much better living as a millionaire's heir in Greece, rather than surviving just above the breadline in London with her.

And the trouble was she couldn't think of a single riposte. All the steam, the anger, the defensiveness had drained out of her. Her protective shell had smashed, and she felt weary and vulnerable.

'Yes,' she said with a sigh, 'I think we can agree about that.'

'Progress at last,' he said mockingly. 'Shall I order some more champagne?'

She shook her head, looking down at her hands still clenched tightly in her lap.

'And you will stay today—for Nicky's sake.'

'Yes,' she said, 'I will—for Nicky's sake.'

They had lunch by the river, a very traditional affair of roast beef and Yorkshire pudding, with strawberries and cream to follow, and Nicky behaved impeccably by anyone's standards. He enjoyed eating, and he also enjoyed being the centre of approving and admiring attention. Harriet recognised rather bitterly that Alex had set out to win his nephew over, and was succeeding brilliantly. She was ashamed of the way she felt when Nicky stretched out imperative arms to his uncle to lift him down from his chair when the meal was over.

A lot of people at neighbouring tables had been watching them during lunch, which Harriet supposed

was inevitable. Even if they couldn't all put a name to
him, Alex was clearly a celebrity of some kind. But
some of their fellow-lunchers had recognised him,
Harriet discovered as she passed the bar on the way to
the powder room.

'This place must be getting fashionable,' an overweight man with grey hair and a moustache was
proclaiming. 'That tycoon fellow Alex Marcos is out on
the terrace with a floozy, and one of his few mistakes in
life, by the look of it,' and he bellowed with laughter.

It would give Harriet immense pleasure to have
emptied his vodka and tonic all over his opulently
waistcoated stomach, but she passed by grimly on the
other side.

The powder room was momentarily deserted, and she
took a long rather weary look at herself. A floozy—and
in particular Alex Marcos' floozy? If it wasn't so funny,
it could also have been sad. Probably by now someone
had enlightened the fat man that Alex Marcos' taste ran
more to voluptuous redheads than to over-slim blondes
in chain store dresses and very ordinary sandals. And
that, of course, when she thought about it—and she'd
done very little else all morning—was why Alex had
turned her down last night.

Because that was what that scene in the bathroom had
been all about—Alex being cruel to be kind, pretending
the onus was on her whether their relationship proceeded
to bed or not when, in fact, he could have said quite
simply that she wasn't his type— that he didn't want her.

He was an experienced man. It wouldn't have taken
him long to deduce the way she was beginning to feel
about him, and that was the last thing he wanted, so he
had decided to administer the death-blow.

It was shaming to think he had had to do it, she
thought miserably. She must have been terribly
obvious. But then she had given herself away that first
evening when he had kissed her. She should have
remembered that he hadn't been motivated by passion,
but by a cynical compulsion to make a point. He had been

determined to make her respond, and he had succeeded
only too well, but now he was drawing the line, treating
her with an aloof and slightly wary courtesy.

It could be worse, Harriet thought with a sigh, but
she didn't see how. She took out her lipstick,
contemplated it, then tossed it back in her bag. To hell
with it, she thought. She was an outsider trying to
compete in a race which was strictly an invitation event.

She left the hotel by the side entrance which led to
the car park. At first she couldn't see Alex and Nicky,
but eventually they came into sight, walking slowly
from the direction of the gardens which sloped down to
the river. Nicky was trotting at his uncle's side, holding
his hand, occasionally giving a little hop of excitement,
and as Alex looked down at the child his harshly
attractive features were softened by a smile.

They were alike, Harriet admitted to herself with a
pang as she stood beside the car, and watched them
approach. With their thick dark hair and olive skins, it
was little wonder that they had been taken for father
and son.

'I'm sorry if we have kept you waiting,' Alex
apologised formally as they joined her. 'Nicos wishes to
give some bread to the swans.'

She made an effort to smile. 'Did he know what they
were? Up to now he's only encountered ducks.'

'Then it is clearly time his horizons were broadened,'
Alex remarked, and Harriet flushed at the implied
criticism.

'By a trip to Greece, no doubt,' she said.

The driver had come round to open the rear door of
the car and was lifting Nicky in. Alex's hand closed
suddenly round her wrist with a grip that hurt.

'Are you still determined to fight me over this?' he
demanded in an undertone.

Harriet looked away, unable to meet his arrogant
dark gaze. 'I don't know,' she said after an unhappy
pause. 'Please let go—you're hurting me,' she added
urgently as his fingers tightened.

He muttered something in his own language and released her, walking round to the other side of the car. The return journey was accomplished in an uneasy silence which Nicky, sitting between them, filled with his own happy chatter about the 'Long ducks'. At any other time Harriet would have laughed and hugged him to her, but now it seemed unwise. He was going to be taken from her, she knew, and her best course was to start letting him go, in her mind at least.

As the car purred through the suburbs, she glanced at Alex. 'Would it be too much trouble to drop me at the flat? I—I'm sure you'll enjoy your afternoon with Nicky far better without me.'

His mouth twisted. 'Saint Harriet the Martyr,' he jibed. 'I think not, however. Nicos might decide to stage another demonstration of how indispensable you are to him.'

'I don't think so. He seems to be much more used to you now and. . . .'

Alex shook his head. 'The moment you are out of his sight he is looking for you, becoming anxious,' he said impatiently. 'He can be diverted, but only for a short time.'

She said colourlessly, 'He stays with Manda—the girl who looks after him while I work.'

'Ah yes,' he said. 'Because he knows that when work is over, you will come for him.'

'You speak as if I were to blame in some way. What was I supposed to do after—after. . . .' She paused, swallowing, recapturing her self-control. 'The authorities suggested I let him be fostered, but I didn't want that. I felt I'd be betraying Kostas and Becca if I let that happen. Are you telling me now I was wrong? How did I know that you were going to arrive, staking your claim?'

'You did not, of course, but you might have guessed,' he said. 'Did Kostas never warn you that what our family has, it holds—for ever?'

'You didn't hold him,' Harriet said unevenly.

Alex smiled cynically. 'He would have returned eventually,' he said. 'When he came to realise how much his little bid for independence had deprived him of, and once his infatuation for your sister had faded, as it surely would have done.'

Her lips were parting to call him a swine when she was aware of a tiny whimper from Nicky. He couldn't grasp the conversation, but he could pick up the vibrations and be upset by them, and Harriet, with a little gasp of compunction, turned away and stared out of the window, her eyes blinded with angry tears that she refused to shed.

Once back in Alex's suite, she excused herself in a small taut voice and went into the bathroom, bolting the door behind her. She bathed her stinging eyes with cool water, and let the tap splash over her wrists, calming her racing pulses. She found it impossible to understand why Alex was so bitter still about Kostas and Becca. Even if he felt, as he obviously did, that his brother had married beneath himself and his family, then surely it couldn't matter any longer.

Harriet sighed, wishing that Alex had met Becca just once. Her vibrant gaiety and charm must surely have captivated him as it had done Kostas.

When she was sure she was once more in control of her temper and emotions, she returned to the sitting room.

Alex was standing alone by the window, staring down into the street below. He turned as she entered, and gave her a long thoughtful look.

'Where's Nicky?' Harriet looked around her, puzzled by the hush which had fallen over the suite.

'Yannina has taken him for a walk,' he said coolly. 'It seemed to me it would be best if we continued our discussion in private.'

'There's nothing to discuss,' she said in a low voice. 'I—I can't win against you. I won't stop you taking Nicky, or make any kind of fuss. It would be selfish to try and deprive him of the kind of advantages you could give him. I've always known that—I just didn't want to admit it.' She swallowed. 'But you will be—kind to him? You won't blame him because he's Becca's child as well as your brother's?'

'My girl,' he said slowly 'what kind of a monster do you think I am?' His voice was icily furious, and Harriet shrank inwardly.

But she lifted her chin, and kept her voice steady. 'What does it matter what I think? It won't make the slightest difference to—to what you intend to do. Will I be allowed to write to him, when he's older—send Christmas presents?'

He said something succinct and violent in his own language and came over to her. 'Sit down,' he ordered, and she obeyed, because she was afraid if she hesitated he might make her do what he wanted, and the thought of being touched by him again, even in anger, was an unbearable one. She thought he might be going to sit beside her, and her whole body tensed uncontrollably, but he remained standing, looming over her, his dark brows drawn together in a thunderous frown.

He said quietly and coldly, 'Yes, it was my intention to take Nicos away—it would be pointless to deny it. But I had not realised then how strong the child's feeling was for you—how necessary you had become to him. It would be an act of senseless cruelty to separate you so absolutely.' He paused. 'So there must be a compromise.'

She looked at him bewilderedly, trying to decide what he meant. Was it possible that he was going to let Nicky stay with her, but contribute to his support?

He said, 'When I take Nicos to Greece, you will have to come with us.'

Harriet had been leaning back against the cushions, but now she shot bolt upright, sending him a horrified glance.

'No!' she almost choked. 'No, I won't. It—it's impossible!'

'How is it so?'

Because I don't want to see you any more, she thought. Because I dare not spend any more time in your company than I have to.

She said, 'Because, as you once reminded me, I have my own life to lead. I have a home—a job. They've been good to me—the company I work for—very understanding, but they're not going to make allowances for ever. And jobs are hard to come by at the moment. And my flat—it may not seem much to you, but. . . .'

'These things—they mean more to you than Nicos?' he demanded coldly.

She gasped, 'Of course not!'

'Then you imagine that if you oblige me in this, I should leave you homeless and without employment?' he asked with contempt.

Harriet shook her head. 'I—I don't want charity.'

'And I do not offer it,' he returned impatiently. 'We shall reach a proper agreement before you leave. . . .'

This was going too fast. She said, 'I don't know yet that I'm leaving for anywhere.'

'Always this resistance!' Alex flung his hands up in a kind of angry resignation. 'When you thought I was prepared to take Nicos from you, you argued. Now I say that you can go with him, and you are still arguing!'

'Put like that, of course, it all sounds so simple,' Harriet said defiantly. 'You make the decisions, and I agree without a murmur. Has it never occurred to you that I might not want my life turned upside down?'

He shrugged. 'Are you saying that it is entirely to your satisfaction? That you have everything you want?' His eyes held hers mercilessly. 'Well?'

'Does anyone have that?' Harriet shifted nervously. 'But that doesn't mean I want to—to throw away everything I've worked for.' She sighed. 'But I can't expect you to understand. Compared with the Marcos Corporation, my efforts must seem totally pathetic. But they're important to me.'

'More important than the wellbeing of your nephew,' he said flatly.

'You know that isn't true!'

'Then there must be some other reason.' He paused. 'Is there, after all, some man you cannot bear to leave?'

'There's no one,' she said, and could have cursed herself for the hastiness of her reply. That was an excuse he might have accepted.

'Then I fail to understand what problem exists, except in your stubborn little mind,' he said. He was frowning again. 'You saw how Nicos was last night. It cannot be good for a small child to be so deeply disturbed.'

'And I can't see how my going to Greece with you would improve the situation.' Harriet stared down at her hands—slim but capable, the nails neatly manicured, a working girl's hands. 'Won't it make matters worse when Nicky and I do part eventually?'

'I do not think so.' Alex shrugged off his jacket, throwing it on the sofa behind him, and loosened his tie before lowering himself almost wearily on to the cushions. 'I shall take Nicos to my home on Corfu. My mother lives there, and her sister. You would stay there for a while and then, as Nicos began to settle, you could perhaps take a few trips—cruise round the other islands—visit the mainland. Gradually he will become used to his new surroundings, and to your absences.'

'Yes,' she said. 'That's—quite practical. And how would you pass me off to your family—as his English nanny? I can hardly suppose I'm going to be very welcome.'

'No.' His mouth twisted wryly. 'But there will be no pretence that you are anything but Nicos' aunt. Any other suggestion would be an insult.'

Harriet sighed again swiftly. 'And how long would you want me to stay?' she asked in a low voice.

If he was pleased at her capitulation, the enigmatic dark eyes gave no sign of it. 'For as long as it takes, Harriet *mou*. No more, no less. How soon can you be ready to leave?'

'I don't know. I'll need a passport. . . .' Her voice trailed away.

He looked at her, frowning incredulously. 'Then you have never been out of England?'

'Never,' she acknowledged. 'Even package tours cost money, Mr Marcos.'

'Alex,' he said autocratically. 'This continued formality of yours is absurd, and will stop now.'

'Yes, sir,' she muttered, and he laughed suddenly.

'You will be the most reluctant guest I have ever entertained! And yet I promise you that you will like Corfu. It has a beauty all its own.'

'So I've heard,' she said. 'Don't they say it's the island that Shakespeare wrote about in *The Tempest*?'

'I believe so.' His smile was slightly ironic. 'Does that increase its charm for you?'

'It doesn't have to charm me,' Harriet said stonily. 'I'm simply going there to do a job. It's Nicky you'll have to sell it to.'

The amusement died from his face. 'Of course.' He was silent for a moment. 'Nicos will need clothing—lighter than you would provide for an English summer, I think.'

'Yes,' she said. 'I won't bring him in rags.'

His mouth tightened in exasperation. 'Harriet *mou*, were you ever slapped as a child, because if you were not, it is a deficit I could gladly repay!'

She was going to say, 'You wouldn't dare,' but as their eyes met, she knew that wasn't true at all. He'd dare all that and more, and her heart lurched suddenly in panic and an odd excitement which stilled the defiant words on her lips.

She said stiffly, 'I'm sorry. I'll buy him whatever he needs, of course.'

'Yes, do that,' he said smoothly. 'I will have Philippides advance you sufficient money.'

She began, 'I can afford. . . .' then subsided, with a weary shrug of her shoulders. 'Just as you wish.'

'You mean that?' he said with soft mockery. 'Another

miracle?' He paused. 'Philippides will help with everything you need. Go to him with any problems that you have—understood?' She looked at him, her expression mutely questioning, and he shook his head. 'No, I shall not be here. You will be relieved to hear that I am returning to Athens tomorrow. But I shall try to get to Corfu in time for your arrival.'

'Yes,' she said. 'I think it would be important for Nicky to find you there.'

He smiled faintly. 'Of course.'

In the corner the telephone rang imperatively, and he sighed impatiently as he got to his feet to answer it, stretching a little as if he was dismissing some lingering tension now that the battle was over and he had won again.

'Only a minor battle,' Harriet thought, her eyes drawn involuntarily by his movement to the lean muscular length of his body. But even so his victory had to be complete. She shivered, watching him cross the room, moving as lightly and gracefully as some big cat. For a man who spent his life directing a huge corporation, he was in good physical shape, she acknowledged, doubting whether he was as much as an ounce overweight. Probably that restless, dynamic energy that seethed in him kept him slim, she thought. Certainly he made the executives in her own company look pale and flabby in contrast.

He said a brusque, 'Yes?' as he lifted the receiver, and then she saw his face change, begin to smile. His voice deepened to a husky drawl, '*Kougla mou*, how delightful of you to call me! No, of course I hadn't forgotten—how could I?' He listened, his smile widening, then said drily, 'You flatter me, my lovely one. As you say—until tonight.'

Harriet stared down at the carpet, listening with a pang to the note of lazy intimacy in his voice. Vicky Hanlon, she wondered wildly, or someone else. Where other men had little black books, Alex Marcos probably had a computer! she thought angrily.

She glanced up and found him looking down at her, his eyes amused as if he could read her thoughts. Her face burned.

She said hurriedly, 'Will Yannina be very long? I really ought to take Nicky home. He—he usually has a nap in the afternoon, and he'll be getting tired and cross.'

'He could rest here,' he suggested softly.

She shook her head. 'It would really be best if we left.' She looked away. 'You have other plans—we'll be in the way.'

'My—other plans are for much later,' he said. 'Why are you in such a hurry to run away, Harriet *mou*?'

'I'm not.' The denial sounded weak even in her own ears.

'There will be nowhere to run to on Corfu.' The dark eyes gleamed wickedly. 'It is a much smaller island than this one.'

'Yes, I know.' She bit her lip. 'You're determined not to make this easy for me, aren't you?'

His smile was grim suddenly. 'I am just preparing you, little one, because on the island it will not be easy at all—not for any of us. Neither my mother nor her sister Thia Zoe have ever forgiven Kostas for—his marriage. You must not expect to hear your sister's name mentioned, Harriet *mou*, and for yourself—I regret that you must anticipate resentment—perhaps even hostility. Are you prepared to suffer these things—for Nicos' sake?'

No, she thought, for yours. Because although it's insanity, and gall and wormwood to have to admit it, even to myself, I'd face a pit full of snakes if it meant seeing you again.

She said quietly, 'Yes—for Nicky's sake.'

And wished with a kind of agonised intensity that it could really be as simple as that.

CHAPTER FIVE

As the plane swooped over the lagoon towards touchdown, Harriet found she was clutching the armrest of her seat until her knuckles turned white. On her lap, Nicky whimpered fretfully, pressing a damp sticky face against her, and she hugged him reassuringly, wishing wryly that there was someone to hug her.

But she could hardly call on Mr Philippides for that, kind and helpful as he had been over the past few weeks. In her heart, she supposed she had hoped that some insuperable obstacle would be discovered that would keep Nicky and herself safely in London, but each minor snag had been smoothed away, almost before she was aware of them. Mr Philippides had been cautious at first, perhaps fearing a repeat performance of that first stormy interview, but gradually his manner had softened, and it was clear he found Nicky enchanting.

Harriet's mouth curved tenderly as she looked down at the small plaintive figure on her lap. He had been incredibly good during the flight, crying only during take-off and touchdown because of the pressure in his ears, but she had been warned to expect this. Apart from that, he had been in his element, and although Harriet had found her first flight frankly an ordeal, she had been careful to conceal this in the face of Nicky's wide-eyed excitement.

Although of course the flight was as nothing to the ordeal which awaited her once they actually landed, she thought ruefully. Mr Philippides in the past couple of days had mellowed sufficiently to drop a few very discreet hints about the kind of difficulties Harriet might be expected to encounter, and Harriet guessed that his guarded comments represented merely the tip of the iceberg.

He was clearly puzzled too about why Alex Marcos had changed his mind about separating Harriet from Nicky. Although he never actually said so directly, he obviously felt that Harriet would have done better to have accepted the generous financial settlement offered by Kyrios Alex, and resigned herself to the loss of the child.

Harriet was touched by the real concern in his eyes as he skirted delicately round the subject, but it did little to support her teetering morale.

She felt very much as if she was being sent into a cage of tigers without even the usual chair and whip to defend herself with.

All over the world, people were marrying other people that their parents neither liked nor approved of, but who were making the best of it, not reacting with the kind of senseless bigotry the Marcos family had displayed towards Kostas and Becca.

She had once tried to broach the subject openly with Mr Philippides.

'But if they feel like that, why do they want Nicky so badly?'

Mr Philippides had shifted papers on his desk in an embarrassed manner and muttered something about 'a male heir'.

'What a pity he wasn't a girl.' Harriet's eyes blazed suddenly. 'Then they might have left us in peace!'

Peace, she thought as the ground rushed up to meet them, routine, monotony. All the things people groaned at and dismissed as boring. She had done so herself, but now she was beginning to realise how precious they could be, how safe and secure.

With a slight thump, the plane was down, and in spite of the warnings to remain seated until it had come to a complete halt, people were already shifting, reaching for hand luggage, preparing themselves for disembarkation, and a fresh babble of chatter had broken out, now that the inevitable tension of the landing had dissipated.

Harriet fumbled in her bag for her sunglasses before she joined the file of people in the aisle. It had been a cool, grey day in London, and here at Corfu airport, the brilliance of the sunlight and the rush of heat once the aircraft doors were opened seemed disturbingly intense and alien.

It was a short walk across the tarmac to the Immigration buildings, and Nicky insisted on walking, giving small excited skips. Harriet wondered if they were being observed from the buildings ahead of them, and moistened dry lips with the tip of her tongue. She had to restrain Nicky from running on ahead, and he wriggled crossly, saying, 'Thio Alex,' as he looked up at her reproachfully.

She hoped he wouldn't be disappointed. Mr Philippides had come with them, she knew, to ease their arrival in case Alex Marcos was too involved in business matters elsewhere. Only the day before they left he had been talking worriedly of problems in New York and Rio de Janeiro.

Immigration could not have been simpler. It seemed to Harriet they were whisked through with just the briefest formalities. Retrieving their luggage took only a little longer.

Harriet was glad Manda had persuaded her to blow her savings on some new lightweight cases, and some new clothes with which to fill them. At least she wasn't arriving like the poor relation. But she had been scrupulous about spending the incredible sum of money which Alex had advanced her through Mr Philippides on Nicky alone, and she had managed to equip him fully without spending even a quarter of it.

Manda had gone shopping with her for her own things, and Harriet knew wryly that she would not have bought half the things folded in layers of tissue in her case without her prompting.

'Beach things,' Manda had decreed. 'And not those ghastly regulation things,' she had added in horror as Harriet had begun to look through a rack of one-pieces.

'You're going to Corfu, for God's sake, not entering for the school swimming gala! You need bikinis—and some of those lovely skirts and shirts to match.'

Harriet's protests that she wasn't going to Corfu for a holiday were brushed aside as irrelevant.

'Even if you're shut up in some nursery with Nicky all day long, there'll be these trips that were mentioned. You can't cruise round the isles of Greece in your office gear. You'll need shorts and tops—and some of those white cotton jeans,' Manda decreed inexorably.

However much she had demurred at the time, and whatever limits her bank balance had sunk to, Harriet was glad she had taken Manda's advice, and was not facing the prospect of confronting the formidable Marcos clan in last year's summer dresses. The outfit she had worn to travel was one of her favourites—a smoothly flared skirt in a cream-coloured silky fabric, with a matching sleeveless top with the low neckline and armholes bound in a contrasting blue. The same blue edged cuffs and collarless neck of the long-sleeved jacket which she had already discarded and was carrying over her arm. She hoped she looked cooler and more composed than she felt.

She heard Mr Philippides greet someone and turned slowly, her heart thumping, to find she was confronting the man who had driven Alex's car in London. He was grinning broadly and scooping their cases up as if they were stuffed with thistledown, as he led the way to the exit.

Nicky ran ahead with Mr Philippides, but Harriet hung back, panic chilling her, closing her throat. She tried to tell herself that it was natural that a car should have been sent for them, it was only common courtesy. It did not—would not mean that anyone else was waiting too.

But he was there. The area in front of the airport was a hive of activity, but she saw him at once through the moving, talking hordes of people. Her eyes sought him as if they were magnetised. He was wearing dark glasses

so she couldn't be sure whether or not he was aware of
her presence or not, but he couldn't be unaware of
Nicky. People turned smiling indulgently as the child
squealed and ran full tilt towards the tall man waiting
by the car. Alex bent, lifting him, swinging him off his
feet while Nicky squealed again with delight.

Harriet's feet felt like lead. She watched Mr
Philippides reach them, observed them shake hands.
Her own hand felt damp and clammy and she wiped it
unobtrusively down the side of her skirt as she walked
up to the little group.

'Welcome to Corfu, Harriet.' His voice was formal,
and so was the smile which accompanied the words.
Any expression in his eyes was hidden by his glasses.
'Did you have a good journey?'

She said faintly, 'Yes, thank you.'

'I hope the remainder of it will be as pleasant. We
have to cross the island to reach my home.'

Harriet silently took her place in the back of the car,
where Alex joined her with Nicky, and Mr Philippides
sat in front with the driver. It wasn't the sort of
limousine he had used in London, but a low-slung
sports-type saloon. As they threaded their way through
the traffic away from the airport, Harriet wondered if it
ever got a chance to demonstrate its full power on the
crowded island roads. Glancing around her as they
drove, she thought she'd never seen as many mopeds
and scooters in her life, most of them carrying two
laughing if not very stable passengers. They were all so
brown and apparently carefree, she thought rather
wistfully, considering the pallor of her own skin, and
she wished she was one of them, just another anonymous tourist with a hotel room and a budget.

She leaned back with a little sigh, stretching her legs
out gratefully in front of her. The plane had been
comfortable but confining, she thought, lifting a hand
and rubbing the cramped muscles in her neck. Aware of
a movement beside her, she turned her head slightly and
realised Alex was looking at her, at the thrust of her

breasts against the silky top which her own action had revealed. Embarrassed, she straightened almost violently tugging, as she did so, at her skirt which had ridden up slightly over her knees. Alex made no comment, but the lines beside his mouth deepened sardonically before he turned away, giving his attention once more to Nicky, who was bombarding him with not always intelligible questions and comments.

Harriet gazed determinedly out of her own window, struggling for control of her hurried breathing. Then gradually the sights and scents and sounds outside the car began to invade her consciousness like a healing balm, and she started to relax. She could understand now why some of the girls she worked with scrimped and saved all year for their few weeks in the sun. It was all so incredibly, exotically different. Heat, she had expected, and dust and rocks, but she hadn't bargained for the frantic beauty of the flowering shrubs, pouring over every garden wall and terrace.

Everywhere she looked there was colour, and even the sheltering greenery had a more vibrant glow. The car turned a corner, and she saw watermelons like great green globes, piled high at the side of the road. For a moment she imagined she could smell them, their clean fragrance invading the overriding smells of exhaust fumes and suntan oil which the faint breeze brought dizzyingly through the open window.

No one actually seemed to be doing any actual construction work, but there were half-built houses everywhere, sometimes only a single storey high, the exposed girders and rods giving them a vulnerable almost skeletal look.

Feeling pressure against her, she looked down and saw that Nicky was drooping wearily, struggling to keep his eyes open, and gently she adjusted her position so that he could slide down putting his head on her lap. She hoped he would sleep, if the car journey was going to be a long one as she suspected it might be. She didn't want his arrival at the Marcos' home to be marred by the kind of tantrum that tiredness and over-excitement often inspired at his age.

Alex and Philippides were conversing softly in Greek, and half her mind registered the unfamiliarity of the liquid cadences as she watched the passing landscape.

The car was climbing now, the tavernas and the souvenir shops left behind, and Harriet was looking at dark pools of olive groves in the sharp decline of the valley beside the road. The air was clearer as they got higher and the breeze held a hint of citrus. The road twisted and almost turned back on itself as it fought the bleak terrain of the hillside, and Harriet found herself trying not to care that the driver hadn't slackened his pace at all, and very much trying not to notice how stark the drop was becoming only a few inches from their wheels.

Alex said, 'Relax—Stavros knows this road well.'

She jumped slightly, because she hadn't realised her tension was so obvious.

She said stiffly, 'Well, let's hope anyone coming in the other direction is equally well acquainted,' and heard him laugh softly.

'Concentrate on the view,' he advised mockingly.

His advice was worth taking. The hills ahead were grey and purple against the unbroken blue of the sky, and deep shadows mottled the valleys. Among the groves, she saw scattered houses with patches of cultivations like wounds in the thrusting vegetation. Donkeys waited in the shade, and tethered goats nibbled voraciously, lifting restless inquisitive heads to stare as the car went by. The blare and bustle of Corfu town behind them seemed a million miles away.

'And not a tourist in sight,' Harriet said, half to herself.

'Oh, they come here,' he said. 'But generally they're just passing through to reach Paleo. This is one of the routes.' He saw her puzzled look and explained, 'Paleocastritsa—it's a holiday resort now, but it is still very beautiful. There is a monastery there too which people like to visit, with some famous icons.'

'Is it near your house?'

He shook his head. 'I live further along the coast—in a comparatively secluded area,' he added, slanting her an ironic smile.

'Naturally,' she returned with equal irony. 'Do you have your own beach as well?'

'Of a kind—not very large and rather rocky.' He paused. 'The descent to it through the gardens is very steep—a mixture of a path and steps. Nicos must not go down there alone, and I have already given orders that a gate must be fixed at the top and kept bolted all the time.'

'Does that mean he can never go down to the beach?' Harriet asked in slight dismay.

'Of course he may, if properly supervised, and the same rule must also apply to the swimming pool.' He shot her a lightning glance. 'Can you swim?'

'Of course.'

'Well enough to teach Nicos?'

'I think so,' she said. 'I had planned to take him to the local baths at home, anyway. They run mother and child classes. . . .' she paused, flushing abruptly as she met his sardonic look.

'At least you have been spared that,' he murmured.

The car was slowing and turning off on to a side road which seemed to Harriet barely wide enough to accommodate it. Citrus orchards pressed on both sides, and the silver glint of olive trees reached across the road in places. And ahead of her, suddenly, she could see the turquoise opalescent gleam of the sea, and she caught her breath. No matter what problems might confront her when she arrived at the house, nothing could detract from the lush appeal of the island's beauty.

The landscape was beginning to change too, cultivation giving way to rioting shrubs, blazing in pinks and crimsons and purples, and as the car wove its way down a steep and winding hill, Harriet saw the sun glinting off a wide expanse of green-tiled roof.

It was like an English garden, only in vivid Technicolor, she thought, looking at the enormous brilliantly green lawns, all with their sprinklers working energetically. The air was heavy suddenly with the scent of roses, and there were beds of them stretching as far as the eye could see, each bush and tree almost bowed down with blossom, the vibrant colours jostling for attention.

The villa itself was something of a surprise—not as palatial as Harriet had vaguely imagined, but lower-built and more rambling, its gleaming white walls hung with vines and creepers which wound their way also round the elaborate wrought-iron of the first floor balconies. In front of the big double doors, a fountain was playing—a stone nymph smiling in remote mystery as she allowed the water to cascade endlessly from the shell she held in her cupped hands.

Apart from the splash of the water, and the constant whirring of the unseen cicadas, it was very still, and the warmth of the sun seemed like a benison as it fell on Harriet's unprotected head.

She thought, 'How beautiful,' and tried to ignore the feeling of apprehension that assailed her at the thought of what might await her behind the cool privacy of those white walls.

She turned to get Nicky, but found Alex had forestalled her. He already had the sleepy child in his arms, and was smiling down at him as Nicky opened uncomprehending eyes and looked around.

The doors swung open, and Yannina appeared, beaming. 'Ah, *pedhi mou!*' Alex swung Nicky to the ground, and he ran towards Yannina with a chuckle of recognition.

Harriet tried to suppress the ignoble pang of jealousy deep within her. She tried to tell herself robustly that it was all for the good, and that the sooner Nicky settled in his new surroundings, the sooner she could be off to get on with her own life.

But what life? Her prospects seemed frankly bleak.

Mr Philippides had spoken of a job being found for her with the Marcos Corporation, but this was the last thing she wanted. Her only hope was to remove herself from Alex's aegis as promptly and completely as possible. The thought of working for him in some obscure section of his empire, of looking forward pitifully to some annual visit where he might or might not remember who she was, was an abhorrent prospect.

She almost started as his hand clasped her arm, urging her forward inexorably towards the open front door.

Inside the villa, she was conscious of space and a blessed coolness which her own rationality told her was air-conditioning. But the décor added something, she thought, as she trod across cool marble floors and looked round at vistas in airy pastels.

There were more double doors in front of her, and they were opening too, and as she hesitated, swallowing nervously, Nicky wriggled free from Yannina and ran back to her, sliding a confiding hand into hers. She gave his hand an encouraging squeeze as they walked forward.

It was a large room, but its focus was solely the two dark-clad figures waiting in the middle of it. Both Madame Marcos and her sister were wearing black, like so many of the peasant women she had spied from the car on the journey here, but their black had the sombre shimmer of silk, and there was a proud glitter of diamonds at throat and wrist. Their eyes glittered too, Harriet realised, with hostility. Two haughty, inimical faces turned towards her.

She felt Alex's fingers tighten on her arm. He said coolly and pleasantly, 'Mama—Thia Zoe, may I present Thespinis Masters, who has brought Nicos to us from England.'

Madame Marcos' firm lips stretched in a travesty of a smile. But her sister was not even prepared for that concession. She glared at Harriet and said something low-voiced and undoubtedly venomous in Greek.

Alex's voice became more pleasant than ever. 'Perhaps we could all remember that Harriet does not speak our language, and only talk in English when she is present.'

Madame Marcos said stonily in perfect English, 'Welcome to our house, *thespinis*.' She made it sound like an insult, but as her eyes settled on Nicky they softened perceptibly, and Harriet fancied she saw a sudden glint of tears, fiercely suppressed.

Nicky was hanging back, pressing himself against her leg. Fierce-looking women dressed in black were something outside his limited experience, and clearly that was where he preferred them. Harriet tried to give him a reassuring smile, but his mouth was already trembling.

Thia Zoe said, 'So this is Kostas' child.' Her accent was more strongly marked than her sister's, and her voice grated slightly. Nicky began to wail, and both the older women stared at him in a kind of dignified amazement.

Yannina pushed forward. 'Pardon, *kyria*, but he is so tired, the little one. *Po-po-po*—all that long journey in a plane! Why should he not cry?'

She picked Nicky up and hugged him.

'He had better go to his room,' said Madame Marcos. 'You also—Thespinis Masters. You have had a tiring journey. Alex, there have already been telephone calls—one from Athens, one from Paris. Perhaps you would deal with them.' The turn of her head away from Harriet was a dismissal in itself.

Yannina said, '*Thespinis,* I will take the little one.' She hesitated. 'I do not know which room you have been given, but Androula will show you.' She nodded towards the elderly woman who had just joined them, also wearing black but with a neat white apron denoting her inferior station.

Harriet turned almost thankfully back to the door. The room seemed to have shrunk to a few square inches, hostility closing round her like a vice.

Yannina's broad form was already disappearing up the stairs with Nicky clasped firmly in her arms. Androula motioned Harriet to follow with an expressionless, 'If you please, *thespinis*.'

The stairs were also made of marble with a wrought-iron balustrade. Harriet's heels clicked emptily as she mounted them. She felt empty too. Her tentative smile at Androula had been met with a total blank, the black eyes impassive as they met hers. There was no real enmity, but she wasn't going out of her way to be friendly either. Clearly she was taking her lead from the mistress of the house, Harriet thought wryly.

Androula led the way along the gallery which looked down on the entrance hall, and turned down a wide corridor, its smooth walls interrupted at intervals by illuminated niches containing exquisite antique pottery. Harriet would have liked to have lingered and examined some of them more closely, but she told herself there was plenty of time for that. Androula led her to a door at the very end of the corridor and threw it open with less than a flourish.

'This is your room, *thespinis*,' she remarked. 'Your baggage will be brought to you.' She gave a curt nod and whisked herself away, leaving Harriet alone to stare round her new accommodation.

For a moment she thought there had been a mistake, or that Androula had had a brainstorm and shown her into a cupboard, but a second glance revealed that there was a bed duly made up, and a chest of drawers and hooks behind the door for those of her clothes which needed to be hung up. There was also, she realised, her temper rising, one very small window up towards the ceiling height, and clearly it had not been felt necessary to extend the air-conditioning towards this particular room, because it was already like an oven.

If she hadn't felt so angry, she would have burst into tears.

She sat down limply on the edge of the bed. This, she supposed, was the equivalent of the servants' quarters,

or possibly even a dressing room, because she now
realised that her bed was standing against a door
leading to the adjoining room. She tried it gingerly, but
it was securely locked, and there was no key to be seen
anywhere. She listened and thought she could hear,
through the woodwork, Nicky's clear high tones, and
Yannina's low-pitched cheerful laugh as she answered
him, and guessed that she was next door to what passed
for the nursery.

She tried to tell herself that this was the room they
assumed she would have chosen, if she had been given a
choice—the nearest one to Nicky's, but it didn't sound
convincing. If this particular room had been at the
opposite end of the villa entirely, it would still have
been allocated to her because it was intended as a snub,
to show her quite plainly how little she was wanted in
this house, how little regarded.

The bed she was sitting on was hard and narrow,
although she supposed if it had been much wider, she
would have had difficulty opening any of the drawers in
the chest, and the pillow, as she touched it tentatively,
felt as if it was stuffed with sawdust instead of down.

She wondered drily whether she was supposed to
protest, to rush downstairs thoroughly miffed and
demand to be returned to Britain on the next available
flight. She shook her head. She was here for Nicky's
sake, not for her own, so she would accept whatever
treatment was handed out without a murmur because at
least she knew it wasn't for ever. This rejection, this
insult of a room would make it all the easier to leave
when the time came, she told herself resolutely.

She decided to go next door and see Nicky, and as
she opened her door, she nearly fell headlong over her
cases, which had been dumped there without a word.
Harriet set her jaw and lugged them into the room.
There was just enough room for the things she had
brought, and she was glad she had remembered her own
dress hangers. It would have been a minor defeat to
have had to ask Androula for some.

She had a smile firmly pinned on when she went into the next room. Nicky, already in his pyjamas, was sitting at a special low table by the window eating his way through fruit and yoghurt, fondly observed by Yannina.

'*Yasoo*, Nicos.' Harriet knelt beside him, accepting the piece of fruit he judiciously held out to her.

'Ah!' Yannina sounded delighted. 'You learn our language, *thespinis*?'

Harriet grimaced. 'A few phrases only,' she returned guardedly. 'Some words, Yannina, from a book I bought in London.'

'You will soon learn,' the other woman prophesied.

I shan't be around long enough for that, Harriet thought.

At least Nicky's room was a proper size, and beautifully cool. The walls were washed in a clear blue, and painted with a frieze of toy animals, and safety gates had been placed firmly across the french windows leading to the balcony. There seemed to be numerous brand-new toys about, and Harriet was relieved to see Nicky's rather battered Paddington Bear leaning against the pillow in his cot. Stick around, she addressed it silently, you could take lessons in hard stares from the ladies I've just met!

While Nicky went on with his food, Yannina led her round, proudly showing her where all his clothes had been put away. There were more toys in a cupboard too, Harriet noticed. There was also a bathroom, tiled in blue and white, which Harriet presumed she was to share. She smiled brightly at Yannina and approved of everything with a heavy heart.

However tired he might be, Nicky was determined not to go down without a struggle. He turned sulkily away from Yannina, stretching demanding arms towards Harriet, saying tearfully that he wanted a story. It was half a dozen nursery rhymes and one and a half versions of the Three Bears later when he finally consented to fall asleep.

As she turned away from the cot, Yannina shook her head at her.

'Ah, *thespinis*, you are so good with him. Good as his own mother, may God rest her soul,' she added, crossing herself.

Harriet was suddenly close to tears again. It was the first time, she thought, that she'd heard Becca referred to with kindness by anyone even remotely connected with the Marcos family.

She said, 'Shall I stay with him for a while.'

'No, *kyria*.' Yannina showed her with pride the wall-mounted microphone which would transmit Nicky's slightest cry to her own quarters. 'It is the time of the evening meal. You will be awaited downstairs.'

Harriet doubted that, but as she emerged from the nursery, it was to see Alex striding down the corridor towards her.

She noticed that he was wearing a dinner jacket, and that he was frowning heavily.

'What have you been doing?' he demanded. 'Dinner is being held back for you. Did Androula not inform you?'

His eyes went over her impatiently, critically, assimilating her crumpled, travel worn appearance, and Harriet smothered a sigh.

'I must have misunderstood,' she hedged. 'Was I supposed to change? I—I've been settling Nicky for the night.'

The frown still lingered. 'Yannina was supposed to do that. It is, after all, your first evening among us. You must not make the child so dependent on you.'

'I'm sorry.' Harriet lifted her head defiantly. 'I thought I was merely doing what was expected of me. If I'm to leave Nicky solely to Yannina then there's very little point in my being here. Would you like me to leave?'

His scowl deepened. 'Believe it or not, Harriet *mou*, I was thinking of you. Perhaps I expressed myself badly. I only arrived back early this morning, and I

am still suffering a little from jet lag. Is Nicos asleep
now?'

She said, 'Yes.' Then, with an effort, 'His—his room
is lovely. I suppose your mother. . . .'

'No,' he said with a faint smile. 'I was responsible for
it. Does that surprise you?'

'A little,' she admitted.

'You thought perhaps that all I wanted was to win.
That once I had control of Nicos, I would lose interest
in him.' He shook his head slowly. 'How little you
know of me!'

Perhaps, she thought, but even that little is too much
for my peace of mind.

She tried to smile. 'Well, I'm sure he'll be happy here.
I'd better wash my hands before dinner.'

Alex nodded abruptly. 'Come down as soon as you
are ready,' he directed.

She watched him walk away, wondering for the first
time if he had planned her room along with Nicky's.
Could it be his own way of showing her how little she
figured in his plans?

Harriet sighed defeatedly and went back into her
room to retrieve her toilet bag which was still in her
case, lying on top of the bed. The only remaining
possession as yet unpacked was a cardboard folder into
which she had placed all the relevant papers and
keepsakes that Nicky might want—his parent's marriage
certificate, his own birth certificate, some letters Kostas
had written to Becca before their marriage, the huge
card he had bought her to celebrate their son's birth,
and some photographs. One of them, an actual wedding
photograph, was in its own leather frame, and with a
kind of defiance she stood it on her chest of drawers.

She didn't bother to change. Keeping the family
waiting any longer for their meal would be just another
black mark against her, she thought resignedly, and
failing to change would simply mean they would think
she knew no better. But she washed her face and hands,
brushed her hair, and applied some moisturiser, along

with a touch of eye-shadow and a discreet modicum of lipstick before she went downstairs.

Androula was waiting in the hall, looking boot-faced. As Harriet came down the stairs, she motioned her towards the same room she had been conducted to when she first arrived.

Her arrival interrupted a heated conversation in Greek which was switched off as abruptly as a radio set as soon as she appeared in the doorway.

Alex was holding a glass containing some pale cloudy liquid.

He said formally, 'Good evening, Harriet. Would you like a drink before dinner?'

She would have loved a drink. She would have leapt head first into a bottle if there'd been one handy, she was so desperate for some kind of courage, but neither of the Marcos ladies appeared to be drinking, so she refused politely.

She looked at Madame Marcos. 'I'm sorry if I've kept you waiting.'

Madame gave her a remote look, and her sister shrugged as if to say it was no more than expected.

Harriet didn't anticipate enjoying the meal. One of the girls who worked with her had warned her that Greek food was usually tepid and everything tasted of olive oil, but the dinner which followed bore no relation to anything Janet had described. It began with an iced avocado soup, and progressed through grilled mullet, to veal cutlets with a delicate wine sauce, and fresh fruit— peaches and melon—for dessert.

Harriet ate with a heartier appetite than she could ever have envisaged under the circumstances. Apart from a few remarks which Alex directed at her, and to which she responded briefly, the meal was conducted in virtual silence.

The atmosphere did not lighten either when they returned to the other room for the tiny cups of thick rather bitter coffee. Madame and her sister produced fine needlework and shared a sofa, sewing and conversing in low voices. Alex had been called to the telephone once again, so as soon as Harriet had finished her coffee, she rose, wished both ladies a polite goodnight which they acknowledged with a frigid nod apiece, and left the room.

'Where are you going?'

Harriet paused on the stairs and looked down. Alex had appeared in the hall below and was staring up at her.

'To my room,' she returned rather defensively. 'I'm very tired.'

'I see.' He sounded sceptical, and she flushed slightly.

'Perhaps—would it make things easier if from now on I had my meals with Nicky?'

'No, it would not,' he said coldly. 'However, if you were too tired to come down this evening and would have preferred a tray in your room, then you should have said so.'

Harriet was tempted to retort that she doubted if there was enough room for a tray, but she kept silent; any such comment could be construed as a complaint, or a plea for better treatment, and she didn't want that.

She said merely, 'I'll remember that in future. Goodnight, Mr Marcos.'

'Harriet *mou*,' he said softly, 'what do I have to do to get you to call me by my given name? I must remind you once more that you are my guest here.'

A strange sort of guest, thought Harriet, shoved into a cupboard, and virtually ignored by everyone from the housekeeper upwards.

She said unsmilingly, 'I'll try and remember that too.'

He was standing just below her, and before she could move, he took her hand from where it was resting on the balustrade and pressed it to his lips. For a fraction of a second she felt his mouth, warm and sensuous against her palm, her fingertips, then she was released.

He said, 'Goodnight, little one. And pleasant dreams.'

He turned away and went across the hall to the room she had just quitted. Harriet stood on the stairs and watched the doors close behind him.

She recommenced her ascent of the stairs wearily, torn between laughter and tears.

He'd wished her pleasant dreams, she thought with irony, when in the same breath almost he had guaranteed her a sleepless night. She paused for a moment, lifting the hand he had kissed and holding it for a moment, achingly, yearningly against her cheek. Then she ran on up the stairs to the cramped loneliness of her room.

CHAPTER SIX

SHE didn't sleep, but it wasn't simply thoughts of Alex that kept her awake. By dint of standing on her bed, she had managed to open her window to its fullest extent, but the little room was still close and airless. She crept into Nicky's darkened—and blessedly cool—room and checked that he was deeply and peacefully asleep before using his bathroom to take a shower, and change into her brief cotton nightdress.

Back in her own room, she stripped the covers from the bed and folded them neatly before lying down, but within minutes she was tossing uncomfortably, hardly able to breathe, her body already damp with perspiration. She considered lugging her mattress through to Nicky's room, but reluctantly decided against it. Yannina might take it into her head to check Nicky during the night, and if she found Harriet there on the floor it would simply result in embarrassment all round. In a hotel, you could complain about your room. In a private house, you had to grin and bear it, Harriet thought bitterly.

For nearly two hours she tried to bear it, although she didn't grin very much. She even tried the insomniac's remedy—to put the hours of wakefulness to good use by writing a letter to Manda. But what was there to say? 'I'm here. No one is friendly, and they've put me to sleep in a sauna.' She decided it would be best to wait until she had something more cheerful to report. Such as 'I'll be home on the next flight', she thought.

She got out one of the paperbacks she had brought and tried to read it. It was a best-selling thriller and in the 'will the world survive this threat of nuclear holocaust?' genre, but as it was set in the recent past and creation was still going about its lawful business instead of lying around in piles of radioactive ash, Harriet found its gut-wrenching propensities so glowingly described on the jacket strangely elusive.

She sat up cross-legged on the bed, lifting her face towards the window and the non-existent breeze, thinking regretfully about the yoga course she'd once planned to take. It would have been nice to have been able to summon up some mantra which would raise her consciousness above such mundane details as being hot and miserable and unable to sleep despite being bone-weary.

At last she swung her feet to the floor with a faint groan. She had to get some fresh air or she would choke. She slipped on the simple peignoir which matched her nightgown, tying the ribbons which fastened it at throat and waist. She didn't bother with the heelless sandals she had brought instead of slippers. The chill of the floor under her bare soles was bliss.

The villa was very quiet. No one besides herself seemed to be stirring, which was all to the good, Harriet thought, as she slipped silently downstairs. She opened the doors leading to the big *saloni*. The drapes had not been drawn over the french windows which comprised one wall, and moonlight flooded the room. Harriet slid her hands down the frame, finding the bolts and drawing them quietly. As she did so, it occurred to her that the house might be covered by a burglar alarm, and she quailed for a moment waiting for flashing lights and alarm bells, but there was only silence, and after a while she breathed again, and opened the window, leaving it slightly ajar.

Except for the lack of colour, the broad terrace and the garden beyond could have been in daylight. Harriet walked to the edge of the terrace and stood breathing deeply and gratefully. It was hard to believe that the cool fragrance surrounding her was the same air which oozed in through her little window.

The cicadas were still busy. The night shift must have come on, Harriet thought, smiling to herself. Just being

outside the villa made her feel happier, more relaxed.
She walked slowly down the terrace steps, and turned
right along a broad paved path. She had no idea where
she was going, only that she had no wish to return to
the house just yet.

The path led right round the villa, she soon realised,
but other smaller paths led off it, one of them to a
tennis court, she discovered. She hadn't played tennis
since she left school, she thought, viewing the court
wistfully, and wondering if she still remembered how.
She sighed. What a beautiful place this was! If only
circumstances had been different she could have been
looking forward to the holiday of a lifetime.

She wandered back to the main path and paused
irresolutely. Somewhere near at hand she could hear the
splash of water. The swimming pool, she wondered, or
another fountain? She followed the sound down a wide
flight of shallow stone steps bordered by rockeries, and
under a stone archway hung with wisteria.

It was the pool, and the arch she had just emerged
from was one of a whole series bordering it, while
directly opposite was a single-storey building with a
tiled roof, and shuttered windows. Changing-rooms,
Harriet surmised in the moment before it occurred to
her that on such a still night there was no reason for
that slight splashing noise. Unless, of course, the pool
was occupied. . . .

Almost incredulously she registered the lean dark
shape cleaving through the water. Noticed other things
as well—the discarded clothing on one of the padded
loungers at the poolside, the bottle and attendant glass
on the table.

Even as an interior voice was warning her that it was
time she was on her way, Alex's hands gripped the side
of the pool, pulling himself lithely out of the water.

Harriet froze, her mouth going dry as she watched
him walk across to the table, refill his glass, then almost
casually reach for a towel and begin to dry himself.

He had a magnificent body, she thought numbly. She

hadn't expected him to be totally naked, but then he probably hadn't expected an audience either. But that she knew instantly, was being naïve. If Alex Marcos wished to swim nude, then he would do so no matter how many people happened to be watching.

But, of course, he still didn't know that she was there. Harriet turned to creep noiselessly away, only to be halted in her tracks by his cool voice.

'Won't you join me? The water's wonderful, and the brandy is French.'

Swallowing, she turned back to face him. The towel knotted loosely round him, he was standing, hands on hips, watching her in some amusement.

She said lamely, glad that her blush didn't show in the moonlight, 'I—I didn't expect anyone to be down here.'

'Nor I,' he returned levelly. 'For a minute I thought you might be walking in your sleep. What are you doing down here?'

'I came out for some air—I couldn't sleep. And the gardens look so fantastic in the moonlight. . . .' Harriet was aware she was beginning to babble, and stopped.

'Earlier you claimed to be so tired you could not wait to get to your room,' he said softly. 'What has kept you awake?'

She gave an awkward shrug. 'I'm just not used to the heat—and my room seemed stuffy.'

He drank some brandy, watching her over the top of the goblet. 'All the rooms are air-conditioned. Or is it something else that you do not know how to operate?'

The sardonic note was not lost on her, and she groaned inwardly.

'If it has been inadvertently switched off,' he went on, 'you need only have rung the bell for Androula or one of the maids. They would have rectified matters for you—although naturally it is flattering that once again you turn to me in your dilemma.'

'I have not turned to you,' said Harriet between her teeth. 'It never occurred to me that you would be down here, or anywhere except your own room, for that natter. I thought you were complaining of jet-lag,' she added.

Alex lifted a shoulder, still gleaming with moisture, in shrug. 'So I was. I came down here with my brandy earlier and fell asleep. When I woke, I decided to take a swim before going back to the villa.' He gave her a cynical smile. 'Had I known I was to have such charming company I would have waited, Harriet *mou*, and we could have swum together.'

She was aware she was being baited, and her fingers clenched tensely in the concealing folds of her peignoir. She said steadily, 'I've tried to explain that I didn't mean to intrude. I think I'd better return to my room.'

'Perhaps you should,' he agreed mockingly. 'But stay and have some brandy with me first.' He poured some into another goblet and held it out to her compellingly, daring her to refuse.

Moving reluctantly, Harriet crossed the short distance from the archway to the table beside which Alex was standing, and accepted the goblet from him. As she took it, his fingers brushed hers and her whole body flinched from the slight contact.

She swallowed, struggling to control the leaping of her pulses. She was playing with fire, and she knew it. The villa no longer seemed an airless prison, but a sanctuary that she wished she had never left.

Alex lifted his glass in silent toast, his dark eyes brilliant with amusement as they slid over her. 'This scene has a certain familiarity,' he said. 'Surely you did not borrow this——' his hand tugged gently at a fold of the peignoir—'from Yannina?'

'Of course not!' Harriet's embarrassment increased with every second. The last thing she wanted to be reminded of was that confrontation in the bathroom in London, and she heard Alex laugh softly as if he could sense her uneasiness. Her fingers tightened round the stem of her glass, and she bent her head to take a hasty gulp of the brandy, letting her hair curtain her face as she did so.

'Gently!' Alex removed the glass from her grasp and replaced it on the table. 'Brandy should be treated with more respect, especially when you are not used to it.'

Harriet felt obscurely irritated by his assumption that five-star brandy was not her usual nightcap. She wished she could have denied it, she wished she could have claimed the sort of sophistication which could take in its stride a moonlit drink with a half-naked man in the caressing warmth of an Ionian night, but it was impossible. She was completely and totally out of her depth, and she knew that he knew it too.

'You—you have a very beautiful home,' she ventured, aiming for a casual tone.

'I am glad that it meets with your approval. Perhaps your stay here will not be such an ordeal after all.'

'Perhaps not.' Harriet's tone was wooden, and she refused to meet his gaze. 'I think I'll go in now.'

He laughed. 'Enough air—enough brandy, or simply enough of me? Harriet *mou*, which is it?'

'A little of each,' she said tautly, and made to turn away, but his hand reached out, his fingers fastening firmly on the soft flesh above her elbow, making her pause.

'What a little coward you are,' he said softly. 'You tried to make me believe you were mature enough to have sole charge of my nephew, but in reality you are little more than a scared child.'

'If that's the case, please let me return to my nursery.'

'Later.' His tone didn't alter. 'When you have learned to be less afraid.'

His skin was incredibly cool under her fainting fingertips as he drew her close.

She said, 'Please—no. . . .' but it was already too late. His mouth felt cool too, but his kiss burned like a brand, searingly possessive. She was trembling, her body pliable as melting wax in his arms, achingly defenceless in her response. Alex moulded her against the length of his body, making her shakingly aware of every inch of bone, sinew and muscle, her sensual consciousness heightened by his lack of clothing. Her lips parted helplessly beneath his demand, her head spinning, her pulses thudding at the sheer ruthlessness of his domination over her. A voice in her head was crying out in protest, even as her senses melted, urging her to accede to anything he might ask of her.

He tore his mouth from hers, muttering something harshly in his own language, then began to kiss her throat, his lips sensuous, caressing the soft skin as lightly as the brush of a feather, lingering with deliberation on her hammering pulse. His fingers tugged impatiently at the ribbon bow at her throat, loosening it, before pushing aside her peignoir and the strap of her nightdress, baring her shoulder to his kiss.

A little husky sigh escaped her as his mouth explored the curve of her shoulder. She felt his hand at her waist, unfastening the other bow, then sliding inside as the edges of the peignoir fell completely apart, down the slender length of her body to her hip. His fingers stroked its gentle swell, then glided inwards and down, discovering the sharp vulnerable line of bone.

Harriet's throat was dry, her whole body poised, almost convulsed with thick excitement. Alex's lips were travelling downwards too, his tongue curling seductively into the hollow between her breasts, making her shiver with pleasure. The voice in her head was silent now, entirely subjected to the need he had aroused in her. His mouth returned to hers in another long, drugging kiss, and she felt his arm glide down under her knees, lifting her off her feet and bodily into his arms. Then she was aware of the softness of cushions beneath her, and realised he had carried her over to one of the nearby loungers, and some semblance of sanity began to return.

He was lying beside her on the wide deeply padded seat, his breathing harsh, his dark face almost terrifyingly intent as he bent over her. Cool, practised fingers slid up her thigh brushing aside the hem of her nightgown.

And suddenly, her excitement was intermingled with panic. It was all too far and too fast—way beyond anything her previous all too limited experience had prepared her for. She snatched at his hand, gasping 'No!'

Alex said softly, 'Don't be a little fool. You knew when you came down here tonight what you were inviting, so why pretend?'

His head lowered towards her. If he kissed her again she would be lost, Harriet thought wildly, twisting away from him.

She said, 'I didn't follow you—I told you why I was here. Please let me go,' she added in a stifled undertone 'Please—Alex!'

His smile was mirthless as he looked down at her 'So—you use my name at last. I wondered what it would take for you to do so, and now I know. But perhaps I do not please. What then?'

Harriet shook her head miserably. 'I—I just don't know. I—I'm sorry.'

'Why? Nothing happened.' His tone was ironic. dismissive, as he turned away from her and sat up. swinging his long legs to the floor. 'Or is that why you are sorry?' he added bitingly.

Harriet's hands shook as she retied the ribbons on her peignoir into untidy bows. 'You know what I meant,' she muttered.

'Yes,' he agreed wearily, 'I know. Let me give you some good advice, Harriet *mou*. Don't create situations you are not prepared—or equipped—to handle.'

'I didn't.' She was close to tears suddenly, knocked off her centre of balance, her emotions in turmoil, and her body hungry for the fulfilment it had been denied. She got to her feet, glaring at him. 'Whether you believe me or not, I did not follow you down here. I came out for a walk because I couldn't sleep and. . . .'

'And you think either of us will sleep now?' he questioned harshly, and she flushed, her eyes sliding away from his sardonic gaze.

'I think I'd better go indoors,' she said in a low voice.

'I think so too—before I forget again why I brought you here.' There was more than a trace of grimness in his voice. He readjusted the towel he was wearing more firmly, then gestured Harriet to precede him through the archway. She hung back.

'I can find my own way,' she protested.

'I don't doubt it, but it happens that I have also had my fill of—fresh air,' he said mockingly.

'You've forgotten your clothes,' she pointed out in a small voice.

'No,' he laughed softly. 'I sleep as I swim, my little English prude. The clothes I took off will be collected, laundered and returned to me later.'

Harriet was fiercely, painfully aware of him as they made their way back to the house. They were the only ones awake, she was sure, but nevertheless it seemed that dozens of eyes were watching them from behind the dark, shuttered windows as they approached. They re-entered the house the way Harriet had left it, and she paused as Alex closed the window and applied the bolt.

'Well—goodnight,' she said awkwardly.

'Not so fast,' he said. 'Don't you want me to show you how the air-conditioning works, or do you intend to spend the rest of the night going for walks in the garden?'

Harriet groaned inwardly. The last thing she wanted was Alex coming to her room on any pretext whatever, but on the other hand she could hardly tell him that the lack of air no longer bothered her when she had made such a point of it.

'Thank you,' she said woodenly. He followed her silently up the stairs and along the gallery to the passage leading to her room.

As they passed Nicky's room, Alex detained her, a hand on her arm. 'Have you forgotten where you are sleeping?' he demanded in an undertone, frowning slightly as he looked at her.

'No.' Harriet shook her head. 'Mine's the next door.'

'The next one?' The frown deepened. 'But that's nothing but. . . .' He stopped as Harriet opened the door, and pushed past her, standing looking around him, hands on hips, in an ominous silence.

At last he said very softly, 'Who told you that you were to sleep here?'

Harriet shrugged. 'It's the room next to Nicky's. I—I was just shown here.'

'Then I must apologise to you. This is not, as you may have gathered, a guest-room. It is small wonder that you could not sleep—or even breathe.' He paused, then said bleakly, 'My orders must have been misunderstood. If you will come with me, I will see that you are accommodated more comfortably for the remainder of the night.'

'Oh, no.' Harriet hung back. 'It's all right, really. I don't mind. . . .'

'But I do,' Alex said inexorably. 'Be so good as to follow me.'

He turned and strode out without bothering to see if she was going to obey or not. For a moment, Harriet hesitated, then reluctantly she picked up her toilet bag and followed him.

She caught up with him, just as he was turning out of the corridor. 'I—I don't want to be too far from Nicky.'

'For tonight that cannot be helped,' he said. 'Tomorrow I will see that suitable arrangements are made for you.'

The room he took her to was on the other side of the villa, and it could not have presented a greater contrast to the one she had just left. It was quite enormous, dominated by a huge divan bed, made up with crisp fresh linen, its handwoven coverlet turned back neatly at the foot. Matching curtains in the same creamy shade hung at the windows, and luxurious fur rugs provided islands of comfort on the cool tiled floor. The bed was surmounted by an elaborate headboard in some dark antique wood, heavily carved and patterned, and flanked by two low tables, their borders and legs carved into an identical pattern. Tall terra-cotta lamps with cream shades stood on the tables, and above each of them, set into the wall, was a console with various knobs and switches, controlling the air-conditioning, the lights, a concealed radio, and even a bell to summon a servant.

'When you are ready for breakfast in the morning, just ring,' Alex directed casually. He glanced round. 'I hope you will be comfortable.'

'I'm sure I shall,' Harriet said rather shyly. 'Thank you, Alex.'

'You have nothing to thank me for,' he said curtly. 'I am only sorry that you should have been given such a poor impression of our hospitality. There will be no more such misunderstandings,' he added grimly, and she knew that he was not merely referring to the room she had been given.

A brief formal 'goodnight' and the door closed behind him. Harriet sank down on the edge of the bed, trying to catch her thoughts and bring them together into some kind of coherent pattern.

She was still shaking in the aftermath of that confrontation beside the swimming pool, her body tingling in expectation of a consummation which would not be realised. She closed her eyes, trying to shutter the memory of the way Alex's mouth had moved against her breasts, the expert feather-light caresses which had brought undreamed of needs into shattering life.

She shivered, running the tip of her tongue over suddenly dry lips. Alex had spoken of misunderstandings—had admitted he had believed she had deliberately followed him to the swimming pool, but could she really blame him for his cynical attempt to exploit the situation? Her denials had been feeble enough in all conscience—and what had she done to fight him off—to convince him that he was quite wrong in his assessment?

Nothing at all, she thought wearily. On the contrary, she had fallen with passionate eagerness into his arms, behaved without pride or self-control—and that was what he would finally remember—not her denials, but the shaming truth of her surrender.

And his own admission that he had momentarily forgotten the reason for her being here on Corfu brought her no comfort either.

Because when Alex touched her, when Alex kissed her, it was all too fatally easy to forget why she was here, to forget all the reasons she had to hate him.

But for her own safety, her own peace of mind, those were the things she had to remember.

Just for a moment, when she woke the next morning, she thought she was still dreaming, and that if she closed her eyes again these brilliantly alien surroundings would shrink and compress themselves into her bed-sitter in London.

But when she looked again, shafts of bright sunshine were still spilling across the tiled floor from between the shutters, and the huge bed still held her in its luxurious embrace.

Harriet sat up slowly, pushing the tumbled hair out of her eyes as the events of the previous night came scrambling back into her mind. An alarmed glance at her watch showed her that it was almost ten o'clock, and rather hesitantly, remembering Alex's instructions, she pressed the bell on the console which would order breakfast.

She climbed off the bed, and picking up her toilet bag wandered towards the bathroom, taking in with amazed appreciation the dark vivid blue of the tiles and appointments, the mirrored walls, and the deep sunken bath. Real colour supplement stuff, she thought, amused by the reflections of half a dozen Harriets all vigorously cleaning their teeth.

The notion of using a bath the size of a small swimming pool was an intriguing one too, and she smiled as she began to look in the cupboards for bath oil.

There were certainly plenty of toiletries to choose

from, she discovered, but all of them had a distinctly masculine orientation. With growing puzzlement, she searched through the remaining cupboards, finding cologne, aftershave, brushes and razors. She slammed the last door, and stood looking round her with a sudden chill of awareness. Up to then, she hadn't noticed the black silk robe hanging on the back of the door, but she saw it now, and she stared at it frowningly, her mind trying to reject the obvious conclusion.

She dismissed the idea of having a bath and walked back into the bedroom.

This was Alex's room, she thought. It had to be. It was the only answer.

There was another door adjoining that of the bathroom, and she opened it and looked in. It was a dressing room, its walls lined with fitted closets. She tugged open the nearest door, registering with almost ludicrous dismay the row of expensive suits it contained.

There was a brief knock at the bedroom door, and a young maid entered carrying a tray. As she saw Harriet, her eyes grew round, and her jaw dropped. It was obvious she believed the breakfast she had brought was for the master of the house, and not for some female guest, and Harriet felt a wave of reluctant colour rise in her face.

Her gaze primly averted, as if she was afraid that at any moment Alex Marcos himself might appear and confirm her worst suspicions, the girl carried the tray across the room and set it down on a convenient table for a moment while she unfastened the shutters and slid back the big glass doors which gave access to the balcony. Then she carried the tray through into the sunlight and set it down somewhere out of sight.

Harriet knew a burning desire to beat a strategic retreat into the bathroom in order to avoid the girl's knowing look on her return journey, but a small interior voice told her that she owed it to herself to stand her ground. After all, it wasn't true, she thought defensively. Nothing had happened. And yet—and yet no one who had chanced to witness their encounter by the swimming pool would ever believe it, she realised with sudden embarrassment.

The maid reappeared, her eyes flickering momentarily to the tumbled width of the huge bed. Harriet's teeth sank into the soft inner flesh of her lower lip, but she managed with an effort to say, 'Thank you.'

'Parakalo,' the girl returned almost indifferently, and was gone. Harriet found herself wondering how many times Alex Marcos had been found with a female companion when his breakfast tray had been summoned. The maid had clearly been surprised at first, but the reason for that wasn't far to seek, Harriet decided ruefully as she glimpsed her reflection in a full-length mirror facing her. She looked ruffled and absurdly young, and not in the least like a femme fatale while her choice of nightwear, although quite pretty, was practical and discreet, rather than glamorous. For a moment, her brows met in a frown of unconscious dissatisfaction, and she lifted her heavy fall of hair on to the top of her head, twisting it into one of the casual knots which she so much admired on other girls but which never seemed to work with her. It didn't really work this time either, she thought with a little sigh. It made her look slightly older, but that was only an illusion. She would never possess the true sophistication that someone like Alex Marcos would look for in a woman.

For a moment she allowed fantasy to run riot, pretending that he was there with her, taking imaginary pins and combs from her hair, and letting it spill softly on her shoulders. She shivered involuntarily, remembering the way his hands had held her, his fingers subtly caressing, arousing, tantalising. . . .

Harriet took a deep uneven breath. That was something she could not afford to remember. To remind herself that Alex Marcos was an experienced man who knew exactly how to make a woman's body respond to him was to do herself a deliberate hurt.

She turned away from the mirror and walked out into the sunshine. The tiles were already warm under her feet as she made her way across to a thickly cushioned wicker chair. She wasn't particularly hungry, but the breakfast awaiting her looked delectable enough to tempt anyone, she thought with unwilling appreciation, eyeing the bread rolls still warm from the oven wrapped in a snowy napkin, with their accompanying curls of creamy butter and assortment of preserves. Freshly squeezed orange juice to begin with too, and to round the meal off, a small wicker basket of huge golden peaches.

Later, as she licked peach juice from her fingers, she realised that she had had more appetite than she thought. All her life, she decided, she would remember this first breakfast on Corfu. Alex's room was situated at the back of the villa and the balcony looked out over the gardens to the sea. The view was incredible. Somewhere there had to be a horizon, but it was impossible to tell where, she thought, as sky and sea blurred together in a distant fusion of exquisite misty blue, while nearer the shore the gentle swell of the water formed an amalgam of colours from jade to azure, and from turquoise to amethyst.

Beneath the balcony, hidden in the riot of flowering shrubs and trees, the cicadas were already raspingly busy, and behind Harriet's head a bee worked with a kind of drowsy industry in the tangle of bougainvillea which clung to the bright wall and draped its brilliant blossom over the balcony rail. The air was full of scents—citrus, roses and warm earth vying with each other.

And this would be Nicky's home, Harriet thought with a pang that she was not ashamed to recognise as envy. This was the beauty which would surround him as he grew up. No more battles with the many uglinesses of city life for him!

And now could Kostas, who had presumably been brought up here himself, have abandoned it with such readiness, settling instead for the very ordinary suburban house he had shared with Becca, and the vicissitudes of the English climate?

Harriet found herself speculating once again on the nature of the rift which had separated her brother-in-law from his family, and left such an incomprehensible residue of bitterness, some of which was bound to spill over towards her. That of course was why she had been given that cupboard of a room. It was a deliberate slight designed to make it plain to her how little she was regarded or wanted. But she couldn't pretend that she had not been warned.

Harriet sighed. This corner of Corfu was paradise, but every paradise had its secret serpent, hiding in the grass, waiting for an opportunity to turn everything sour, to pervert and destroy.

Alex said, 'You look very serious, Harriet *mou*. What are you thinking?'

She twisted hastily on the cushions. He was lounging against the window opening, casually dressed this morning, she noticed, in pale linen slacks and a dark short-sleeved sports shirt unfastened almost to the waist.

He said smoothly, 'I came and helped myself to some clothes earlier. You were asleep, so I was unable to ask your permission. I hope you passed a comfortable night.'

'Oh, extremely comfortable.' Her tone was ironic. 'That of course was before I realised that I was sleeping in your bed.'

His mouth still smiled, but his eyes hardened. 'Are you afraid you have been contaminated in some way? Allow me to reassure you. The room may have been prepared for me, but I've only used it to shower and change my clothes.'

'That isn't what I meant,' she said hurriedly. 'I'm objecting to the fact that you gave the room to me. It wasn't necessary.'

'You think not? I am afraid I must disagree with you,' he said coolly.

'What I mean is—there must surely be other rooms. By putting me in here, you've placed me in a very difficult position. I—I don't know what your staff—your family will think.'

'They already know exactly what to think, because I have made the position more than clear to them.' His glance was almost contemptuous. 'And—yes, of course there are other rooms, but none of them were prepared last night as this was. Or did you wish me to wake Androula and the maids in the middle of the night to make an alternative ready for you? Finding us together at that hour, dressed—or rather undressed as we were—might have begun exactly the kind of speculation you seem so anxious to avoid.'

'Yes, I see that,' Harriet said reluctantly, beginning to wish she had said nothing.

'I hope you do,' Alex returned sardonically. 'If it will placate your fear of scandal, perhaps I should say that your new room should now be ready, and I will call Androula to conduct you there.'

He was making her sound like a prude and an idiot, she realised with exasperation. However real her embarrassment had seemed to her, it was clearly foolish to him. But it was impossible for her to try and explain the reasoning behind her objection in case unwittingly she gave too much away.

Avoiding his glance, she said stiltedly, 'I'm sorry—but the maid—she clearly thought ... I mean, it was obvious it wasn't the first time....' She halted in total confusion.

'Not the first time I have had a woman in my room—in my bed?' he finished for her with awful courtesy. 'I won't deny it. Why should I? But let me assure you that my—companions of the night have all been women and not immature children incapable of knowing their own minds—or their own bodies. Does that satisfy you?'

Harriet felt as if she had been slapped across her face.

In a thickened tone, she said, 'Perfectly. Now, if you would be good enough to call your housekeeper, I'd rather like to get dressed.'

The dark eyes swept her lightly covered body with casual lack of interest, then Alex lifted one shoulder in a shrug which told her quite explicitly, without any further words being needed, that it would make no difference to him if she were stark naked.

Then he turned, and she heard the sound of his stride taking him across the room, and the distant slam of the bedroom door.

Harriet sank back against the cushions, staring unseeingly in front of her as the glorious view dissolved into a thousand shimmering fragments. Convulsively she closed her eyes, refusing to let the painful tears fall.

Only a few moments ago she had thought she was in paradise. Now she knew to her cost just how bitter paradise could be.

CHAPTER SEVEN

By an almost superhuman effort, Harriet was still managing to control her unhappiness when a frankly sulky-looking Androula came to fetch her a few minutes later.

Hardly had they left Alex's room when the woman began to chatter in her own language. Harriet couldn't understand what was being said, but she could recognise recrimination and self-justification when she heard it. It was obvious Androula had received a tongue-lashing from the master of the house over the standard of the accommodation assigned to his guest, and Harriet guessed wryly that a rough translation of Androula's remarks would have amounted to the fact that she was only obeying orders.

The room she was taken to was only slightly smaller than the one she had just left, and lacking nothing in luxury. When Androula had taken her still-aggrieved departure, Harriet discovered that her clothes had already been brought and unpacked for her. It was such a contrast to the treatment she had received the previous day that she could almost have laughed out loud.

That is if she hadn't been feeling so miserable, she amended inwardly.

But she wouldn't have been natural if she hadn't experienced some lift of the heart brought about by her new surroundings. She took a long, warm, scented bath, then dressed in cool, simple clothes—a cotton wrap-round skirt featuring giant poppies on a navy background, and a navy cotton tee shirt, short-sleeved and scoop-necked.

She was stroking a brush through her hair when there was a knock at the door, and a beaming Yannina ushered Nicky into the room.

'Oh.' Harriet dropped the brush and held out her arms to him. 'I was just coming to find you.'

He scrambled on to her lap, burying his face in her shoulder. 'I find you,' he said in a muffled voice.

'He slept well, *thespinis*,' Yannina informed her. She shook her head. 'But he would eat no breakfast.'

'Oh, Nicky!' Harriet gently detached his clinging hands. 'You must eat your meals.'

The small face was mutinous. 'Don't want it,' he muttered. 'Too hot. Don't like it.'

'Just wait a day or two,' Harriet soothed him. 'It will seem as if you've been here all your life. We're going to have a wonderful holiday—a lovely time with Uncle Alex. You'll see.'

She had to resist the impulse to hug him to her fiercely. This was all part of the letting-go process she was committed to. It had to be. But it would be so easy to play the traitor—to encourage Nicky in his quibbles about his new surroundings, to re-establish herself as the indispensable factor in his life. It would be easy— and balm for the ache inside her. But in the end, what would she gain?

Yannina was intervening, smiling again. 'Come, little one. Kyrios Alexandros is waiting to see you. We must not keep him waiting.'

Heaven forbid, Harriet thought savagely, picking up her brush and attacking her unfortunate hair as if it was a dirty carpet.

She said, 'I'll see you later, Nicky. Perhaps we'll have a swim in the pool, hm?'

Nicky assented cautiously, and went off hand in hand with Yannina.

As the door closed behind them, Harriet expelled her breath on a little sigh as the unnaturally bright smile faded from her lips. Oh no, the next few weeks were going to be so hard—worse than her most pessimistic imaginings. The gradual parting from Nicky would have been bad enough alone, without this foolish, ill-judged passion which Alex had engendered in her, and the overt hostility from the Marcos women.

She supposed reluctantly that as the morning was half over, it was more than time she presented herself downstairs. She rose and looked at herself critically in the mirror, fiddling with the sash tie of her skirt, and an errant tress of hair. But she was simply procrastinating, she knew, and there was no point in trying to present herself as some kind of fashion plate when, to the women downstairs, she would never be anything more than Nicky's poor relation.

She was able to take in more of her surroundings in the warm, golden light of day, and she found the cool, spacious layout of the villa very much to her taste, accented as it was towards simplicity, the walls washed in plain colours, and natural fibres used alongside stone and wood.

When she arrived in the hall, all the doors opening from it were shut, and the place seemed deserted apart from one maid sweeping the floor. When she saw Harriet, the girl propped her broom against the wall and gestured that Harriet should accompany her, leading the way towards the room where Madame Marcos had received her the previous evening. Harriet wiped the suddenly damp palms of her hands down her skirt, tension filling her at the prospect of another inimical encounter, but when the door swung open there was only Mr Philippides, putting down the newspaper he had been glancing through and rising to meet her with a broad smile.

'*Kalimera*, Thespinis Masters,' he greeted her. 'I am so glad to have this opportunity to say goodbye to you before I return to London.'

'You're going back?' Harriet was dismayed. Mr Philippides was the closest she had to an ally in the house, apart from Yannina, and she had hope he would be there to help her through the first awkward days.

'I must, *thespinis*.' Perhaps Mr Philippides sensed her disquiet, because he looked at her sympathetically. 'I have meetings planned—business to transact which has already had to be delayed.'

'I didn't realise you'd made a special journey to escort us here,' Harriet said slowly. 'I—I'm sorry to have put you to so much trouble.'

'No trouble, but my pleasure, Thespinis Masters. You and the little Nicky will be safe and happy here in the care of Kyrios Marcos. It is a beautiful house, *ne*?'

'Very beautiful,' Harriet acknowledged woodenly. 'But at the same time I think it was a mistake for me to come here. Would—would there be room on your flight for me, do you suppose?'

Mr Philippides gave her a shocked glance. 'You distress me, *thespinis*. It would be an insult to Kyrios Marcos to leave so soon.' He paused, and gave an almost furtive look round to ensure that they were not being overheard. 'If you are disturbed by the coolness of your reception by Madame Marcos and Madame Constantis—this I can understand. It is very difficult, but I am sure that if you are—patient, then the situation will improve.'

'Thanks for the reassurance,' Harriet said caustically. 'I'm glad you understand what's going on, because I certainly don't. And if his mother and his aunt have these sort of feelings, then perhaps Mr Marcos should think again about bringing Nicky up here.'

Mr Philippides sighed. 'You—and the child, Thespinis Masters—are a reminder of an unhappy time in their lives. It will take time, but the ladies' attitude will mellow, I am sure. Or at least towards the little Nicos,' he added with a slightly apologetic note in his voice.

And if it ever mellows towards me, it isn't too important, because my stay here is only temporary anyway, Harriet supplied wryly and silently.

Aloud she said, 'But why do they feel like this, Mr Philippides, do you know?'

He looked instantly embarrassed, moving his shoulders defensively, and murmuring something about a private family matter, but Harriet was unconvinced.

Their dealings in London had shown her that Mr
Philippides enjoyed a high degree of Alex Marcos'
confidence, and there wouldn't be many family secrets
kept from him. But such trust implied an equal amount
of discretion, Harriet realised with a little inward sigh.
Whatever secret had poisoned Kostas' relationship with
his family, and still shadowed his memory, it was a
mystery from which she was excluded.

And yet for Becca's sake, and perhaps more
importantly for Nicky's, she felt it was something
which should be solved. Yet not, she thought
regretfully, through the agency of Mr Philippides.

She thanked him colourlessly for all his help in
escorting her to Corfu, and for his kindness to them
both, and said a quick goodbye, escaping out through
the patio doors because she could hear female voices
approaching through the hall.

Coward, she apostrophised herself when she was safely
out of sight of the villa. You should have stayed and faced
them, and demanded an explanation. She smiled then
ruefully, trying to imagine anyone demanding anything of
the stately Madame Marcos. Oddly enough, she thought,
it was the vindictive-seeming Madame Constantis who
seemed the less formidable of the pair, perhaps because
her hostility was so open. Under Madame Marcos' cool
civility, Harriet had detected something implacable and
chilling. Perhaps Alex hadn't inherited all his ruthlessness
from his father.

She stopped and looked round her almost curiously,
as if it had suddenly occurred to her just how alien this
environment was from any experience she had ever had.
She liked flowers. She had always kept plants in her
room at home, but there wasn't one brilliant shrub
thrusting its way out of the raw-coloured earth that she
could have put a name to. It was all new and strange,
and she was alone in the midst of it.

She felt the strength of the sun beating down on her,
and suddenly shivered as if a cold wind had blown on
her, or an unknown hand touched her shoulder.

Harriet reached for the bottle of oil and began to smooth another coating over her legs. Her tan was coming along nicely—even and golden brown, but that, she thought drily, was hardly surprising as she had little to do but work on it over the past two weeks.

For the first few days of their stay, Nicky had been querulous, shy of the new faces and unaccustomed attention, and fractious because of the heat and change of diet. Harriet had been able to feel that her presence at the villa was at least justified, but now she was not so sure. Nicky had begun to turn more and more to the devoted Yannina for his needs, and Harriet had realised ruefully that much of the time he was hardly aware if she herself was there or not. But she couldn't blame him if that was so, she kept reminding herself. That, after all, was the whole purpose of the exercise, and it seemed that Nicky's settling down process was going to be more painless than they could ever have hoped or anticipated.

But when she had suggested quite diffidently to Alex that this might be a good time to take her departure, she had received a brisk rebuff.

Nicky, his uncle thought, was merely charmed by the novelty of his surroundings and Yannina's uncritical solicitude. Sooner or later the novelty would wear off, and Harriet's presence would be necessary to him again.

Harriet had attempted to argue the point, spurred on by her own private reasons for not wishing to remain on Corfu a day longer than she had to, but Alex had only grown coldly angry.

'I thought that you were devoted to Nicos' well-being, or so you would have me believe when we met in London,' he said with icy sarcasm. 'Why are you now so ready to shirk your responsibilities?'

Harriet gasped. 'I'm not shirking anything,' she responded warmly. 'I simply don't feel I'm fulfilling any real purpose by remaining.'

'You will kindly allow me to be the judge of that.'

Alex gave her a bleak look. 'And it is my wish that you remain here—until the end of the month at least,' he added, forestalling the further protest which was already trembling on her lips. 'I have to go away on business tomorrow, so perhaps we could delay any further discussion until my return.'

She had assented reluctantly, unable to subdue a swift inward pang at the news that he was going to be absent, even for a short time. Her own feelings aside, Alex was very much a bulwark between herself and the unvarying hostility still evinced towards her by his mother and aunt. Even in his presence, family mealtimes were an ordeal where she was made to feel like an unwanted outsider. It was subtly done, of course. There had been no repetition of the tactics which had led to her being allocated a room which a servant might have occupied.

Harriet had guessed from the tension in the atmosphere during the first few days of her stay that Alex had made his views on that more than clear. She was more than happy with her new room, and thankful for it too, because the heat was such that she knew she would never have got a moment's sleep in the other room, but at the same time she wished Alex had never found out, because the resultant fuss had just given his family something extra to resent her for.

It was absurd to feel hurt or even disturbed about that, but she did. She liked people, and she always had. She had had plenty of friends at work, even if her social life had become rather curtailed because of Nicky. She had written a number of letters since she had been at the villa, all of them giving glowing accounts of her surroundings, making it all sound more fun than it actually was. Not even to Manda had she confessed how miserable she really was. Not that she thought for a moment that anyone at the villa would actually go to the lengths of steaming open her correspondence to see what she was saying, but because her unhappiness was somehow more bearable if she didn't think about it too much. Writing about it might crystallise it in her mind, and make her life here totally unbearable.

It was easier to keep up the pretence that she was having a wonderful holiday in the sun in a particularly beautiful corner of the world. A very restricted corner, she reminded herself wryly. All she had seen of Corfu, apart from the initial trip across the island, was the villa garden, and the small beach which she had made her ultimate refuge.

There was little wonder that Alex had placed an embargo on Nicky going down there, and reinforced it with a gate which had to be kept bolted at all times. The path leading down there was little better than a track, steep and stony with a few rock steps provided here and there to assist with the worst bits and a wooden handrail. Even so anyone using the path needed to be surefooted and have their wits about them, and Harriet usually went down there in the middle of the day, after lunch when Nicky was having his siesta.

There was a small jetty on the beach, and a boatshed containing a sleek, racy-looking speedboat, as well as a variety of water-skiing and windsurfing equipment. Harriet supposed that Alex used them, but she didn't know when. It was certainly never when she was down at the cove.

She really hadn't had to worry at all about avoiding him, because it was all being done for her. Until they had clashed over her proposed return to London, he had been unfailingly civil, but always aloof, making it tacitly but positively clear that there would be no more love-making even of the most casual kind.

Harriet tried to tell herself that she should be grateful for this, because if Alex had ever decided to amuse himself by pursuing her in real earnest, then she could be in more trouble than she had ever dreamed of. And he was a man in need of amusement, she could be in no doubt of that. The even tenor of life at the villa could not hold him for long. There were few visitors, and when they did come, they were mostly older couples, friends of Madame Marcos and her sister.

Alex went out a great deal in the evenings, and Harriet was unable to blame him. She was thankful she had brought a bag of paperback books with her to occupy her, usually retiring to her room immediately after coffee was served each evening. Sometimes she was woken, her room being at the front of the house, by returning headlights, and she knew without even consulting her watch that it was the early hours of the morning, and that Alex was home at last.

None of the defensive arguments against him that she had managed to marshal could still the ache of longing deep within her which assailed her every time she saw him. Watching him swimming in the pool, or lying relaxed in the sun with only the minimal covering on his bronzed body, or even catching an occasional breath of the cologne he used as he went past her—all these things had the power to stir her, to rouse passionately bitter-sweet memories.

If she'd belonged to him, if she'd known what it was like to make love with him, then sleep in his arms, she couldn't have been more physically conscious of him. The strength of her emotions, the force of her awareness bewildered her. She'd never felt like this before. She didn't know how to handle it, how to subdue her feelings.

She had thought about love, of course. She had had other boy-friends apart from Roy, and when she had seen how happy Kostas and Becca were together, she had looked forward from courtship to a marriage of her own, because even in these uncertain days it seemed that love and security were still possible and attainable.

It had been a calm, peaceful optimism about the future, but she knew now that with Alex, she wouldn't care that there could never be any future just as long as there was a 'now'. She was ashamed of feeling like that. She had discovered depths within herself she had never suspected, an ability to desire, to need which had shaken her totally. In this alien place, far from home, she seemed to have become a stranger to herself.

She capped the sun-oil bottle and lay back on the sun-lounger, deliberately making herself relax as the warmth of the sun caressed her limbs, listening to the somnolent whisper of the sea, only yards away.

It was difficult to keep troubled thoughts at bay at times like this when solitude pressed on her. No one had suggested that she might like to do any sightseeing while she was here. Well, she could hardly expect an offer from Alex to show her the island in the circumstances, but his wasn't the only car, and the driver who had brought them from the airport wasn't overworked. But she couldn't ask. Any offer would have to come from Madame Marcos, and would be as unlikely as a sudden snow shower, she thought ruefully. Madame clearly felt that sunbathing most of the day, and playing with a small child, was the most her unwanted visitor could ask for, and Harriet knew that for many people, a fortnight in these surroundings with nothing to do and all day to do it in would be a dream holiday.

But she wasn't one of them. She felt restless and on edge. She had thought Alex's absence would make things easier, but she was wrong. The tension of actually being in his orbit was more than equalled by the tension of wondering what he was doing and when he would return. I can't win, she thought, half-closing her eyes so that the sun was a golden shimmer through her lashes.

And now she had at least an hour to spend before she need rouse herself and go up to the villa to see Nicky. Who could ask for anything more? she thought with self-mockery, knowing already what the answer was. She wanted so very much more, and yet, if they were offered, she would settle for crumbs instead of the proverbial half-loaf.

She was dozing lightly when she heard the sound of footsteps coming down the path. Her eyelids flew apart,

and she sat up, propping herself on one elbow. A man's
step. It couldn't surely be Alex. She had no idea how
long he was going to be away, but she had formed the
impression that it could be measured in days rather
than hours. And though there was Andonis who
worked mainly at the beach, seeing to the boat and the
gear, he wasn't usually around in the afternoon.

No, the newcomer was a stranger to her. Young,
male, wearing a towelling beach jacket over brief
trunks. He was shorter than Alex, and stockier, with an
apparently ready smile which he was aiming directly at
her. As he approached, Harriet felt ridiculously that her
black bikini was too revealing and half-reached for the
thin shirt she had adopted as a cover-up between the
villa and the beach, then stopped, telling herself firmly
that she was just being prudish.

He reached her side and stood looking down at her.
'Thespinis Masters?' His voice was more heavily
accented than Alex's. 'I am Spiro Constantis. My
mother told me that we had the pleasure of your
company here for a few weeks. She did not warn me,
however, that you used this beach in the afternoon. I
hope I do not intrude.'

Then where do they imagine I get to each day—
disappear back into the woodwork? Harriet managed to
refrain from saying.

Aloud, she said 'Of course not. I suppose I should
ask you the same thing, Kyrios Constantis.'

'Spiro, if you please.' He pulled up another lounger
and sat down. 'And I will call you Harriet, *ne*? It is so?'

Harriet supposed it was. He seemed pleasant enough.
Compared with his maternal relations, he seemed
positively charming, but for a reason she found it
difficult to analyse, she didn't want to seem too
forthcoming.

Spiro discarded his jacket, squinting appreciatively at
the sky.

'A beautiful day—and a beautiful companion to
share it with. I am fortunate. Usually if there is female

company at the villa, I have to compete with my cousin Alex, and that'—he shrugged with self-depreciation— 'is no contest at all.'

Harriet smiled rather stiffly. She had no need to be reminded of the electrifying effect Alex had on women. She had seen it operate in London, seen the glances which often couldn't even bother to be discreet or sidelong as he went his arrogant way.

Collecting her thoughts hurriedly, she asked if Spiro worked for the Marcos Corporation.

'Indeed yes—in the Athens office, but I was owed a few days' leave, so I thought I would come here and meet my new little cousin.' He sighed. 'Poor Kostas' son. What a tragedy!'

Harriet looked away, towards the sparkle of the sea. 'I thought it was,' she said steadily. 'I loved Kostas, and my sister Becca was a super girl. They were very happy.'

'That is a good thing to know,' Spiro said softly. 'When he was younger, he caused my aunt many anxious hours.'

'Oh?' Harriet's brows lifted. Kostas might have had wild oats to sow in the days before she had known him, but she could have sworn he had never given Becca as much as an anxious moment. She paused, then said rather woodenly, 'Then it's a pity she never found out what a good effect his marriage had on him. I—I suppose if it hadn't been for the accident, they'd have eventually been reconciled.' She made it into a question, and Spiro's smile faded as he considered it.

'Perhaps,' he said at last. 'Kostas was her favourite son, even if he was not—a satisfactory one. But I do not think—forgive me—that my aunt would ever have received your sister. She felt—she still feels great bitterness. You must understand that she felt— betrayed, and that your sister contributed to that betrayal.'

Harriet gasped. 'In what way, for heaven's sake?' she demanded indignantly.

Spiro looked uncomfortable. 'You do not know? But

I thought—I was sure that you would have been in your sister's confidence. Pardon me, I should not have spoken.'

'No—please.' Harriet spoke urgently. 'If there's something I should know, something which would help me understand, then I would prefer to be told.'

He gave a slight shrug. 'Perhaps, but I do not feel it is my place to tell you. Alex is the head of the family, after all.'

'Don't we know it,' Harriet muttered, and his gaze sharpened.

'So there has been—friction between you. Ah, poor Harriet, but it was inevitable.' He paused, then said flatly, 'It might have been better if you had not come here.'

'I had very little choice,' Harriet said defensively. 'Your cousin wanted to make Nicky's transfer to his new life and surroundings as easy as possible, and so. . . .'

'I see.' Spiro looked at her sympathetically. 'He is not with you today, the little Nicos?'

'No.' Harriet shook her head. 'I don't bring him down here often. The path is too steep and dangerous, for one thing, and he finds the sea rather overwhelming after the shallow end of the pool.'

'But he can swim?'

Harriet smiled. 'After a fashion. He loves splashing about.'

'You are clearly very fond of him. He is a fortunate child. To have the devotion of so lovely a girl and then—one day—to own all this.' He waved his hand around him. 'Unless of course Alex grants his mother's dearest wish by marrying and having children of his own,' he added casually.

Harriet experienced a pang so sharp she nearly cried out. The thought of Alex with another woman, looking with pride and satisfaction at the son she had borne him, was frankly intolerable. And she would know about it. There was no escape from that. The marriage

of Alex Marcos, the birth of an heir to the Marcos
Corporation, were events which the gossip columns of
the world would hardly fail to record. But at least she
wouldn't have to be here to see it. She'd be a thousand
miles away, making a life for herself, trying to expunge
the bitter-sweetness of this Corfu summer from her
mind, something she had to do if she was ever to have
any peace again.

She said with an admirable attempt at coolness, 'He's
hardly likely to remain single.'

Spiro grimaced. 'He has escaped so far, but my aunt,
I think, hopes that he will make amends to the
Xandreou family by marrying Maria.'

'Why should he do any such thing?' Harriet asked
with unguarded sharpness. She immediately tried to
dissemble. 'I mean, it's a pretty drastic way of making
amends.'

'Not,' Spiro said gently, 'to the girl whom Kostas
jilted to marry your sister. Something else you did not
know, ne?'

'I didn't know he was actually engaged.'

Spiro shrugged. 'There was an understanding—an
arrangement between the families. It was as binding, or
should have been, as a formal engagement. Kostas'—
defection was a humiliation for both families.'

Harriet could feel sympathy with this unknown
Maria, but at the same time she had never found it in
her heart to blame Kostas for escaping while he could
from such a cold-blooded arrangement. And no one
who had seen him with Becca, who had experienced
their happiness would have blamed him either, she
thought.

Except here. Here there was resentment, and a deep-
seated grudge which might have hung over their lives
and cast a shadow over that happiness.

She said slowly, 'So now there's another—
arrangement with Alex?'

'Of a kind. Alex has never been the marrying kind,
but he has a keen sense of family honour, and Maria is

his mother's godchild, so they are often in each other's company.' His mouth twisted slightly. 'She is coming to stay here tomorrow, so you will be able to judge for yourself.'

Wonderful, Harriet thought wretchedly. Just what I want.

Aloud, she said, 'It won't be much of a judgment unless I see them together—and Alex is away.'

Spiro laughed. 'That is true—but he will return. You will see, little English Harriet.'

She forced herself to smile in return, as if he had said something very amusing. 'If he's prepared to cut short a business trip, then he must be serious.'

Spiro was still laughing. 'A business trip? Well, it is an excellent excuse. A little family life here at the villa is enough for Alex. Sooner or later he becomes bored, restricted, and he takes off for brighter lights. He has a mistress in Athens, you understand.'

She was hurting again badly, which was ridiculous because a man like Alex would have women wherever and whenever he wanted them. She couldn't pretend the news came as any surprise, she thought, remembering that phone call at the hotel in London, and Vicky Hanlon's voluptuous charm.

She said brightly, 'I hope his future wife doesn't know.'

Spiro's mouth twisted. 'Maria is a sensible girl. She would consider turning a blind eye to Alex's other interests a small price to pay for becoming the new Madame Marcos—for marrying the Marcos millions.'

'Then they should be perfect for each other,' Harriet said grimly. A small price, she thought incredulously. If she were in Maria's place, even the slightest hint of infidelity on Alex's part would be like losing a piece of herself.

If he was opting for marriage, it was small wonder he had decided on an arrangement with a Greek girl who would be 'sensible'. The last thing he would want would be a wife who clung and complained, and demanded all his attention.

'You are very quiet,' Spiro commented. Harriet looked at him and saw him watching her, his eyes frankly assessing her body, its curves barely concealed by the scraps of bikini. She had a ridiculous impulse to cover herself with her hands, because she suddenly realised she didn't want Spiro looking at her. In fact it occurred to her that although he was good-looking and seemed friendly, she didn't really like Spiro very much, but that was probably because he had told her things she didn't want to hear. They had executed messengers who brought bad news in the old days, and, just at the moment, it seemed like a good system.

She said stiltedly, 'I'd better go back to the house. Nicky will be waking up.'

'And he likes you to be there. I cannot blame him.'

The words sounded fulsome, and she said, embarrassed, 'He's only a baby really. For a while, I was all he had.'

He laughed. 'Of course. I said he was a fortunate child.'

She smiled uncertainly, reaching for her shirt and pulling it on, even fastening a couple of the buttons. Her hands were steady enough, but she was shaking inside.

She needed to get to the house, to her room, so she could fall to bits in private.

Spiro said, 'I hope to see you later,' and she mumbled something in reply as she made for the path. Once on it, she made herself slow down, picking her way carefully because she didn't want to fall, and it was too hot for running anyway.

I can't run, she thought. There's no escape. No way out. I'm trapped here until Alex chooses to release me. And tomorrow she'll be here—this Maria—and he'll be here too, and I shall have to watch them together.

She wanted to lift her hands in despair to the sky, shout something savage at the sun, but she knew she could still be seen from the beach, knew without turning her head that Spiro was watching her departure, so she thrust her balled fists into the pockets of her shirt, and went on climbing, her head bent, and her eyes fixed with a kind of desperation on the rough stones beneath her feet.

CHAPTER EIGHT

'RUN, run as fast as you can——' Harriet paused, waiting for Nicky to join her joyously in the second half of the couplet. '"You can't catch me—I'm the gingerbread man!"'

But there was no response and when she looked at him, Nicky's small face was unsmiling, his bottom lip pouting slightly.

Harriet sighed. 'I thought you liked this story.'

'Don't want a story,' he said rebelliously. 'Want swimming.'

Harriet closed the book, and put it to one side. She'd tried all his favourites—The Little Red Hen, Three Billy Goats Gruff—in turn, but all to no avail, yet usually he listened entranced.

She had decided against the swimming pool that day because Yannina had reported that Nicky had been coughing a little in the night, and she thought herself he looked a trifle flushed as if he might be developing a slight temperature. But Nicky had become accustomed to his daily splash in the pool, and had made it clear from the outset that staying indoors and being read to was no substitute at all.

He seemed perfectly all right again too, she thought, eyeing him, with not a trace of a cough or a sniffle. There really seemed no valid reason to deny him his wish, and keep him in the villa—except. . . .

This time her sigh was inward. Except that Maria would be down at the pool, she thought wryly, and that was an ideal motive for keeping as far away as possible.

She had made all kinds of resolutions before Maria's arrival, mentally rehearsing the way she should behave, the things she should say, but she had wasted her time. Because from the moment she had entered the villa a week earlier, Maria had made it quite clear that she shared the view of her hostess, and that Harriet, and to a lesser extent Nicky, was less than the dust beneath her chariot wheels.

They had been introduced—Spiro had seen to that—and Maria had looked her over briefly and frowningly, then turned away after a perfunctory greeting which fell little short of overt rudeness. After that she behaved for the most part as if Harriet did not exist.

But in that, Harriet admitted drily to herself, her behaviour was a little different from the remainder of the household. No one wanted her there, and in Alex's absence they took little trouble to conceal it. Conversation at mealtimes was conducted wholly in Greek, and the only time that English was spoken to any extent in her presence was during Nicky's daily sessions with his grandmother, from which Harriet excused herself as often as possible.

Watching Madame Marcos struggling to entertain the child formed a poignant contrast to Harriet's memories of her own mother. Rachel Masters would not have sat on a sofa, stitching tapestry and holding a stilted conversation with a largely uncomprehending Nicky as he played at her feet. She would have been down there with him, among the building blocks and wind-up toys, uncaring about her appearance or dignity, and Madame Marcos, Harriet thought, was someone who would be positively improved by a little tomboyish ruffling.

In many ways, it was sad, because at times she watched Nicky with real yearning in her eyes. But although she insisted that he should be brought to the *saloni* each day after his afternoon nap, she still held him at arms' length, and in his turn Nicky regarded this black-clad stranger with caution still.

But at least he did not show her the aversion he felt for Madame Constantis. He had called her a witch once, but fortunately only Harriet had heard, or at least understood him. Harriet wondered sometimes if

Madame Marcos could have relaxed more with the
child if her sister had not constantly been present,
inhibiting her. Madame Constantis made no secret of
the fact that she did not approve of Nicky's presence in
the household, and the reason was not hard to guess at,
Harriet had realised with wry amusement. With Kostas
gone, the doting mother had decided that her Spiro was
the rightful heir if Alex persisted in remaining a
bachelor, and she openly resented the small intruder
who had upset her cherished plan.

She acquitted Spiro of sharing his mother's ambitions.
He seemed half embarrassed, half amused by some of
her pointed remarks, and he more than made up for her
marked indifference to Nicky.

In fact, Harriet had found herself warming to him as
the days went by. His simple, uncomplex personality
was a much-needed palliative to all the other tensions
and hostility in the villa, and she realised that her
earlier reservations about him had only existed because
she was unconsciously comparing him with his cousin,
to his detriment.

But she had ended up liking him in his own right,
particularly because of his unswerving friendliness in
the face of his mother's disapproval. And it was
amusing to watch Madame Constantis' unsubtle and
unavailing attempts to get him to desert herself, and
pay all his attention to Maria.

Madame Marcos might have decided that she would
be the ideal bride for Alex, but it was clear that her
sister thought the Xandreou heiress would suit her own
son much better. And it was equally clear that Spiro
wanted no part of it.

Maria was a pretty girl, Harriet fair-mindedly
admitted, and she would have been even more attractive
without the petulant expression which marred her
features so often. She had a spectacular figure which
she showed off to the best advantage in a series of
minuscule bikinis, each with its matching wrap or
pareu. Even her sandals, with their incredibly high

gilded heels, matched, as did the soft kid bags in which she carried her cosmetics and sunglasses.

Maria Xandreou, in fact, Harriet decided, was not short of the good things in life, and liked the world to know it.

Each day she appeared at the pool, oiling herself lavishly in order to deepen an already immaculate tan, but she never went into the water. But that, Harriet thought maliciously, was probably just as well, because Maria was so loaded down with gold chains and bracelets—round her neck, her waist and her wrists and ankles—that she would have sunk like a stone.

The greatest exertion she seemed capable of was looking through glossy fashion magazines—probably seeing pictures of Vicky Hanlon, if she did but know it—and Harriet wondered why she didn't go out of her skull with boredom. But hers not to reason why, she decided, and meanwhile it was better for her to concentrate on keeping Nicky well out of Maria's way, because she made it obvious that the noise of his play and chatter irritated her.

Nicky tugged at her hand. 'Swimming, Harry,' he pleaded, and whooped with pleasure when she reluctantly nodded. As he ran ahead of her into the sunlight, Harriet followed slowly, wishing there was some alternative delight to tempt him with.

Maria was already ensconced on her lounger when they arrived, the flowered sun umbrella adjusted to the correct angle, and a tray with a tall jug of iced fruit juice placed conveniently to hand on one of the tables.

She sat up as they approached and removed her sunglasses.

All the better to glare at us, thought Harriet, giving the other girl a swift impersonal smile as if she hadn't noticed a thing. She peeled off the simple cotton shift she was wearing and draped it over the back of one of the cushioned chairs stationed near the shallow end of the pool. Nicky, dancing with excitement, allowed her to remove his tee-shirt, then darted towards the steps leading down into the water.

Harriet sat on the tiled edge, dangling her feet in the water, and watching indulgently as he threshed about energetically. When he got tired, there was a huge inflatable swan for him to ride on—another evidence of Alex's thought. Nicky adored it, and often insisted on bringing some bread down from the house so that they could ceremoniously pretend to feed it.

Eventually she joined Nicky in the water, encouraging him to float on his back, and then to swim with proper strokes, all the time aware that Maria was watching them, her face set in lines of annoyance.

As she lifted him out at last, and wrapped him in a towel, she was not altogether surprised to see Maria beckoning imperiously.

She gave Nicky a quick hug. 'Dry your hair,' she urged in an undertone, then picking up her own towel she walked to where Maria was lying.

The Greek girl's eyes looked her over from the pale damp strands of hair on her shoulders, to her bare feet, taking in the white towelling chainstore bikini on the way.

She said glacially, 'Who gives you permission to use the pool at this time?'

Harriet frowned. 'I don't understand you, *thespinis*.'

Maria's chin lifted in affront. 'I speak very good English. You do not want to understand. I say you should not use the pool, or bring the child down here, when there are guests of the family present. The boy is noisy. Take him back to the nursery now, *parakalo*,' she added offhandedly.

Harriet felt a blaze of temper rise within her, but her smile didn't waver. 'I'm afraid that it's you who does not understand, *thespinis*. I am not Nicky's nanny. I'm his aunt, and I'm also a guest here.'

She didn't believe for a moment that Maria wasn't perfectly well aware of the relationship, but if she expected her to look discomfited, then she was disappointed.

Maria's shrug was negligent. 'There is a beach,' she said. 'There he could make as much noise as he wishes. Why do you not take him there?'

Harriet held on to her patience. 'Because the path down to it is dangerous for someone of his age. Alex has had a gate fixed to the top to prevent him from straying down there, as you may have noticed.'

She saw Maria's eyes narrow at the use of Alex's name, and went on hurriedly, 'I'm sorry if Nicky disturbs you, *thespinis*. Perhaps you aren't used to small children and. . . .'

'I am perfectly accustomed to them,' Maria said icily. 'Many of my friends are married, but Greek children are taught to behave properly, to play quietly. English children seem to me spoiled, and allowed to become— hooligans.' She pronounced the word with a kind of triumph.

Harriet said quietly, 'Nicky's half Greek, if you remember,' then wished she hadn't, as she saw a flash of real hatred in Maria's dark eyes. Every time Maria looked at Nicky she must be reminded of Kostas, and the fact that he had jilted her, she realised, and there was no way she could convince the other girl that her last remark had not been a deliberate jibe. She suppressed a sigh and said, 'But if you really find him such a nuisance, I'll take him elsewhere.'

Maria gave a slight shrug, implying that Harriet could take him to the ends of the earth with her goodwill.

At that moment Spiro came striding under the archway. He was casually dressed in shorts and a leisure shirt, with espadrilles on his bare feet, and was carrying a camera.

He halted when he saw them. 'Ah, you have already been bathing,' he said with evident dissatisfaction. 'I came to see whether you and Nicos would like to go with me to Paleocastritsa. Behave like tourists for a day, *ne*?'

Harriet forbore to remind him that, as far as it went, that was really all she was. She couldn't prevent a surge of excitement at the invitation, remembering that Alex had described Paleocastritsa as one of Corfu's beauty spots, but to escape from the environs of the villa for a while, she felt she would have jumped at a chance to tour the local gasworks.

She said smilingly, 'That would be lovely. Nicky, we're going to the seaside in Thio Spiro's car! That is—it is the seaside, isn't it?' She turned to Spiro in sudden doubt.

He laughed. 'Indeed it is. A fine beach, although very crowded, and a bay with tall cliffs and many caves. You will like it there.'

Harriet scooped their belongings together and hustled Nicky towards the villa, promising to be as quick as possible. She was sure she would like Paleocastritsa, and the glimpse she had got of the look of baffled temper on Maria's face had added an extra dimension to her anticipated pleasure.

Maria, she was sure, had no intentions of swapping Alex for Spiro, in spite of his mother's machinations, but at the same time she clearly felt that any invitations which were going should be aimed at her, rather than a little English nobody.

It was ignoble to feel triumphant, but she did.

While Yannina attended to Nicky, Harriet showered rapidly, and changed into another bikini, topping it with a one-piece playsuit in a pale lemon stretch fabric, and pushing her feet into simple leather sandals.

Spiro's eyes lit up with admiration as she came downstairs, holding Nicky's hand.

'How beautiful you look,' he said. 'Let us go quickly.'

'Before anyone sees us?' Harriet supplied drily, and he gave her a quizzical glance, and a faintly embarrassed shrug.

'You are in an unfortunate position in this house, Harriet,' he said when they were in his car and on their way.

Harriet sighed. 'You don't have to remind me! But I still don't see why. Kostas wasn't the first man in the world to marry someone his family didn't approve of, and he won't be the last.'

'That is true,' Spiro acknowledged. 'But it was not only the marriage——' He stopped short, as if aware he might have said too much, and Harriet turned to him impulsively.

'Please go on—I think I have a right to know what's going on, as I'm the one who's principally affected by it.'

Spiro looked uncomfortable. 'Perhaps, but Alex would not be pleased, I think, if I were to discuss a close family matter with. . . .' he hesitated.

'An outsider,' Harriet suggested woodenly. 'Of course, I could always ask him—telling him that you'd whetted my curiosity.'

'I hope you will do no such thing!' Spiro looked horrified, then laughed. 'Oh, very well. As you say, you have a right. I have seen how my aunt behaves towards you, and it is not kind.'

Not to mention your own mother who, of course, has been charm itself, Harriet thought with irony.

Aloud she said, 'Forgive me, but does Madame Constantis know that you're taking us to Paleocastritsa?'

He nodded. 'It was partly her own idea. You must understand, Harriet, that it would have given me much pleasure to have taken you out before, only. . . .'

'Only it might have upset too many people,' she said quietly. 'Are you quite certain you didn't misunderstand what your mother said to you?'

'You do not believe me? Well, I suppose I cannot blame you. You must understand that my mother is a woman who feels very deeply, both love and hate. Since the death of my father, she has been living here with my aunt. As they are widows, it is a good arrangement for them, but since she has come here my mother has become too concerned with'—he looked embarrassed again—'certain aspects of our family relationship.'

'You mean she saw you as Alex's heir.' Harriet stared at the tall sombre lines of a group of cypresses.

Spiro groaned. 'It is so obvious? I feared so, and yet it is ridiculous. It is inevitable that Alex will marry and have a son. Even if the little Nicos did not exist, it would be so. My father, you know, was not a poor man, but always my mother has had this envy of the Marcos family, and of her younger sister who made this brilliant marriage. It is sad, but it is part of her nature.'

'Didn't any of them know that Kostas had had a son?'

'Alex knew, but said nothing, until his brother's death made it necessary for him to act, of course.'

'Well, that's something we aren't likely to agree on,' Harriet said drily. 'But why did Kostas quarrel with his family?'

Spiro sighed. 'I spoke of my mother's envy. Well, it is something from which the Marcos family themselves are not immune. And poor Kostas envied his brother. Alex was the oldest—and from childhood he had this power—this charisma. Kostas was always in his shadow, and he resented it. Thus, when he joined the Corporation, he tried certain—innovations, tried to pursue a line independent from Alex, who at that time was already the Chairman. But he lacked Alex's flair, his aggression in business dealings, and he failed badly, as Alex had warned him he was likely to do. Alex was very angry, as you can imagine, and harsh things were said.' He sighed again. 'Kostas was given an ultimatum—in future he was to—toe the line, and as a first step he was to marry Maria as it was the wish of both families that he should do so.' He paused heavily. 'There was a terrible scene, and he walked out. Eventually he went to England, but to work independently of the Marcos Corporation. That must have been when he met your sister.'

'Yes, he had a job in an accountant's office.' Harriet smiled wryly. 'When he told Becca who he was, I don't think she believed him.'

'Ah,' Spiro said. 'Then perhaps he acted as he did to convince her.'

Glancing at him, Harriet saw that his goodnatured face was grave. Trying to speak lightly, she asked, 'Well, what did he do?'

Spiro paused for a long moment, then said heavily, 'He stole a ruby ring from his mother to give to her.'

Harriet's lips parted in a gasp of sheer amazement. She glanced round at Nicky, but he was absorbed in a picture book on the back seat, and probably would not have understood the trend of the conversation anyway.

She said flatly, 'I don't believe you.'

'It is unhappily most true.' Spiro sent her a sympathetic look. 'It distresses you, I see, and I can understand it. It was not an action worthy of him, and it hurt my aunt deeply. It was a long time before she could bring herself to speak his name. Again, it is a sad story, full of anger. Kostas came here to the villa to tell his family that he was going to marry your sister, and to ask his mother for the ring which she had promised him for his future wife. It was to be a gift, you understand, for the bride. But my aunt refused to give it to him, stating that your sister was not the wife she had chosen, and she would not recognise her as such, that his marriage was an insult to Maria Xandreou and her family—oh, many things were said, as you can imagine.'

Harriet shuddered. 'Yes.'

'Kostas also said many things, accusing his mother of cherishing Alex as her favourite, of always preferring him. He said that unless his family agreed to receive your sister as his wife, he would have nothing more to do with them, that he would leave the next day, taking with him only what he was entitled to. There were certain documents, a precious icon which had been a present from his own godfather, all in the safe in Alex's study—where his mother's jewellery also was.'

Harriet didn't think she wanted to hear any more, but she knew that, having started this, she had to.

Spiro went on, 'The following day after he had left, it was realised the ring had gone. Alex, I think, would have followed him to London, made him give it back, but this my aunt would not permit. But it was your sister that she blamed in her heart. She said many times afterwards that Kostas would never have done such a thing unless this woman had prompted him.'

Harriet shook her head wretchedly. 'But there was no ruby ring. I remember the icon, because Kostas sold it when Nicky was expected to pay for all the things that were needed. But Becca never had any jewellery except her wedding ring, and her watch. Oh—and a little gold pendant with a pearl in it that Kostas bought her for Christmas.'

Spiro shrugged. 'Then he must have sold it also. There can be no other explanation.'

'But what did he do with the money, if so?' Harriet demanded. 'They never had any extra cash. Becca was even glad of what I could pay as rent when I lodged with them.'

'I cannot answer these questions. Again and again I have asked myself what made Kostas do such a thing, but I have never found an answer which gave me satisfaction.' His mouth tightened. 'I thought I knew him too—we were of an age—and I would have sworn it was not in his character to do such a thing—to hurt his mother so much, no matter how deeply they might have quarrelled.' He gave her a sidelong look. 'Perhaps he was ashamed afterwards and kept the ring somewhere, never daring to show it. In a safe deposit, maybe?'

'I'm sure he didn't.' Harriet was vehement. 'He was upset about the quarrel with his family, but that was all. And the theft of a valuable ring from his mother of all people would have preyed on his mind—made him miserable. I know it would. And he wasn't miserable. They were both so happy.'

'You are a loyal and affectionate friend, little Harriet.' Spiro smiled a little. 'But the evidence is—overwhelming.'

'I don't care a fig about evidence,' Harriet said roundly. 'I know Kostas was no thief, that's all.'

'Well, you and I will not quarrel about it,' he said hastily. 'There has been too much sadness and too much anger in the past, and perhaps it is best that this part of it remains a mystery.'

Harriet didn't think it was best for a moment, but Spiro was her host, and when he determinedly changed the subject to the changes he had seen overtake the island since his boyhood, she went along with him. But the shine had gone out of the day for her.

She was shocked to the core by Spiro's account, because although she had not the slightest doubt of Kostas' innocence, it was nevertheless a fact that a very valuable piece of jewellery had vanished, and that someone must have taken it. And if further enquiries had been passed over, it followed that Alex and his mother must have had good reason for thinking Kostas was the culprit.

One of the servants? she wondered. It seemed unlikely. She had already learned from Yannina that all of them had been with the family for years, apart from a couple of the young maids who were recent arrivals— far too recent to be implicated.

She asked herself whether Kostas knew what he was suspected of, and remembering his bitterness and his reluctance to discuss the rift with his family, thought it was only too likely.

As Spiro had prophesied, Paleocastritsa was teeming with people when they arrived. They parked the car and walked along the road beside the beach, Nicky becoming the proud possessor of a toy windmill purchased at one of the roadside stalls.

It wasn't an enormous bay, the high brooding cliffs giving an enclosed effect, but its deep green waters were alive with wind-surfers, swimmers and water-skiers. There were little ramshackle wooden jetties too, extending out from the beach where larger boats plied for trade, offering trips round the sea caves. Harriet would have loved to have gone on one of these, but Spiro did not suggest it, and she suspected that such unsophisticated entertainments were probably beneath him. But he was a good companion, solicitous for their comfort, insisting that when they reached the sea wall at the end of the bay they should stop at one of the tavernas there for cold drinks.

Nicky had an enormous glass of orange and amused himself by trying to drown the ice cubes with his straw. When he tired of that, he wandered to the edge and sat gripping the railing, and watching some children playing with buckets and spades in the sand below.

Finally he announced gleefully, 'That lady's bare!'

Harriet turned quickly and found him pointing at an impressively topless beauty sauntering along at the water's edge. Spiro snorted with amusement, his gaze following her with frank appreciation.

'They start early in your family,' Harriet muttered, turning back to her drink.

'In these days it is unavoidable.' Spiro drank some beer, still looking amused. 'You do not approve, Harriet?'

She flushed a little. 'I—I just know that I would never have the nerve to do it.'

'I am grieved to hear it,' Spiro said politely. 'You will be surprised to hear that my cousin Alex shares your disapproval, but for a very different reason. He believes that a woman's breasts should only be uncovered for the eyes of her lover, and that she loses much of her mystery by exposing herself thus to the gaze of any passer-by.'

'Oh, does he?' Harriet was crossly aware that the colour in her face had become more pronounced and that Spiro was observing this with interest. 'How very old-fashioned of him!'

Spiro chuckled. 'Shall I tell him you said so—when he returns?'

'He doesn't seem in any great hurry to do so.' Harriet

grasped a straw that might lead the conversation back to the general.

Spiro grimaced. 'I cannot find it in my heart to blame him. If it was my fate to marry Maria, I too would stay away as long as possible.'

'Nonsense,' Harriet said stonily. 'I'm sure she'll make him a very good wife. Come away from those railings, Nicky, you're going to bang your head.'

To Harriet's delight, they got their boat-trip after all, Spiro indulgently sharing their pleasure as the boatmen guided his craft between the gleaming pinnacles of rock, and in and out of the dark grottoes where sea-urchins and starfish were clearly visible in the crystal clarity of the blue water, and shoals of tiny fish darted in and out.

Afterwards they ate at a taverna on the hillside above the bay, sitting on a vine-covered terrace, sharing a messy but satisfying platter of shellfish while Nicky made his way solemnly through an omelette. Spiro introduced Harriet to *retsina*, a clear golden wine tasting of resin which, after the first few sips, she found curiously palatable. They finished the meal with coffee and bowls of dark purple grapes, while Nicky chased butterflies in the garden below, and tried to persuade a thin and suspicious kitten to play with him.

When the meal was ended, they joined the other sunbathers on the sand, Nicky relapsing without protest into sleep in the shade of a large sun-umbrella which Spiro fetched from the boot of the car. Harriet stretched out beside him and closed her eyes, but she couldn't sleep.

Her mind kept reverting to the things that Spiro had told her earlier. No matter how hard she tried, it was impossible to keep them at bay. They were there, like corrosive acid, eating into her contentment, her peace of mind. She felt as if the shadow of the accusation made against Kostas had touched her too through Becca, and through Nicky. How could he grow up in this place among people who were ready to believe that his father had been a thief?

Was this what invaded Madame Marcos' thoughts each day when Nicky was with her? Remembering how deeply she had been hurt by the father, did she hesitate to give unstinting affection to his child? It seemed an inevitable conclusion to draw, and if it was true then surely even Alex could be made to see that it was better for Nicky to return to England rather than be brought up in such a shadow.

Her eyelids flew up as Spiro leaned over her and gently tweaked her foot. 'You look sad, Harriet, and this is not a day for sadness.' He paused. 'Do not fret over things you cannot change. Let us swim.'

The water felt gloriously cool and silky against her skin, and it buoyed up her spirits as well as her body as she swam and turned and floated, as carefree suddenly as a dolphin while Nicky shrieked and splashed at the water's edge.

She was more resigned, if not wholly at peace, as they drove home in the later afternoon, Harriet sitting in the back of the car with Nicky, his salt-sticky curls reposing on her lap as he dozed.

As the car came to rest by the front door of the villa, Yannina appeared as if by magic, beaming. '*Kalispera, thespinis*. It has been a good day, *ne*?'

'Very good.' Harriet was smiling as she passed Nicky over to the older woman's waiting arms. 'Tea, and then bed, I think, Yannina.'

'I think so too, *thespinis*.' Yannina vanished into the shadowy interior of the house, and Harriet was about to follow when Spiro detained her, a hand on her arm.

'The day does not have to end here,' he urged. 'Have dinner with me tonight. We could drive to Nissaki— there is a taverna there overlooking the sea. Say you will come with me!'

Harriet hesitated, sensing danger. Spiro had established himself firmly in her good opinion during the day, but that was as far as it went, or ever could go. There was a note in his voice which warned her that his interest might be deepening beyond a mere desire for companionship, and this worried her.

On the other hand, she could not deny that yet another fraught meal *en famille* had very little appeal, particularly as, in spite of Spiro's assurance, she was wondering how Madame Constantis might regard her day out in his company.

She said slowly, 'It sounds marvellous, Spiro, only. . . .'

'Only I must be sure not to get any wrong ideas,' he finished for her, his face frankly rueful. 'So—who is the fortunate man, because there must be one. Not, I hope, my cousin Alex,' he added sharply.

Harriet was terrified that a betraying blush would confound her, but by some miracle it did not come, and she was even able to manage a light laugh.

'Of course not! I'm not a complete fool. Casual womanisers just aren't my scene. No—there's someone in London. His name's Roy. I—I expect we'll be married when I go home.'

Spiro sighed, lifting his shoulders in a little shrug. 'Nevertheless, Harriet, I would very much like to take you to dinner. With no strings—if that is what you wish.'

'In that case, I'd like to have dinner with you. Thank you, Spiro.' On an impulse, she reached up and kissed him, brushing his swarthy cheek swiftly with her lips.

He grinned teasingly. 'Is that the most I can hope for?' He bent towards her, and found her mouth with his. It wasn't a passionate embrace by any standards, but she was still beginning to pull away—even before Alex's voice said curtly from the doorway behind them, 'I obviously intrude, may I suggest you choose a less public place for your lovemaking?'

Harriet whirled, gasping, her hands flying up to press against her warm cheeks.

She said shakily and ridiculously, 'Oh, you're back.'

'How perceptive of you.' The harshness in his voice didn't soften, and the nod he gave Spiro was glacial. 'You have wasted no time, I see, cousin.'

'Following your own example—*cousin*,' Spiro came back at him lightly.

Alex's mouth tautened, and he said something in Greek which brought a dull flush of angry colour to Spiro's face. He started forward impetuously, but Harriet intervened, appalled.

'Oh—please!' She clutched at Spiro's arm. 'Please don't spoil my day.'

He paused, then shrugged almost sulkily, muttering something about putting the car away. He walked round, slamming into the driver's seat, and shot off with a screech of tyres that lifted a cloud of dust from the drive.

Leaving Harriet alone with Alex.

It was a wide doorway. Three people could probably have passed in it quite comfortably, yet his lean body seemed to be a sudden impassable barrier.

She passed her tongue round dry lips and said, 'Would you—excuse me, please.'

He said with ominous quiet, 'I wish to talk to you.'

'About Nicky?' She stared at the ground. 'Oh, he's fine. We—we took him to Paleocastritsa for the day. You were quite right—it is beautiful there.' Aware that she was babbling, she allowed her voice to fade into silence.

'Does Nicos invariably accompany you on your sightseeing tours with my cousin?'

She was about to point out that this had been the one and only trip she had made in Spiro's company, when a sudden gust of anger shook her. After all, she was supposed to be a guest in this house, not a servant or a prisoner. And no one was going to put Alex through a similar inquisition about his activities in Athens, she told herself furiously.

She lifted her chin. 'Not always,' she said coolly. 'For instance, he won't be going with us this evening when Spiro takes me to dinner at Nissaki. Now, if you'll excuse me, I should be getting ready.'

She expected him to move out of the way, but she

was wrong. The dark head was flung back slightly, and his eyes glinted arrogantly at her.

He said, 'But I do not excuse you anything, Harriet *mou*. And as it seems you have become so prodigal with your kisses in my absence, then the least you can do is welcome me as I would wish.'

His hands descended on her shoulders, pulling her inexorably towards him, and his mouth ravaged hers with slow sensual expertise. She clung to him, her fingers clenched round the soft folds of his shirt. He needed a shave. His chin rasped against her skin and she shivered, feeling her body dissolve in longing against his. When he lifted his head, and that fiercely pagan sting of his fingers on her flesh relaxed, a whimper of yearning—of protest that she could not control, was torn from her tight throat.

He said softly, 'Now go to Spiro.'

She could not move. It was he who turned and went, leaving her alone on the threshold.

It seemed very quiet suddenly, the air hushed and heavy with the advent of evening, even the cicadas silent. All she could hear was the splash of the fountain behind her, and she turned and looked at the nymph, remote and smiling on her pedestal, and realised that she too knew what it was to be turned to stone. But instead of the nymph's distant, unearthly smile, on her face there would have been tears, frozen there for all eternity. . . .

CHAPTER NINE

THE heat was almost stifling, Harriet thought, lifting her hair away from the nape of her neck with a little sigh. The slight languid breeze from the sea only stirred the air without cooling it, and each day seemed more oppressive than the last.

But this, she supposed, was why most people came to Corfu for their holidays—for the promise of this kind of brilliant, cloudless weather. And if she herself were merely a holidaymaker, she would probably be loving it too, she thought.

She had no right and little reason to feel so miserable, she told herself over and over again. By anyone's standards, she could be said to be having a wonderful time. Spiro had seen to that. She had explored the island in his company, visited the town, seen the shrine of Saint Spiridion in his own church where his mummified body reposed in a silver coffin, driven round the streets in an open-air carriage trimmed with bells behind a horse in a straw hat, watched cricket being played on the dusty square on the Esplanade, and shopped for souvenirs in the narrow crowded streets to the strains of the ever-present *syrtaki* music.

They had picnicked in coves, accessible only by boat, and Harriet had had her first tentative lessons in water-skiing in the bay below the villa, a smiling Andonis manoeuvring the boat while Spiro shouted instructions from the stern.

Each night she went to her room healthily tired with sun, sea and exercise, and each night she tossed and turned, unable to sleep, because it was only when she was alone that she was able to think, and the thoughts which came were as dark and oppressive as the nights themselves.

Alex obsessed her. Since the evening of his return, she had gone to great lengths to avoid being alone with him, but she couldn't ban him from her waking dreams, and he was the reason she found sleep so disturbingly elusive.

Not that he was so difficult to avoid during the day, she thought bitterly. That sudden, wild blaze of passion might only have existed in her imagination. Sometimes when she responded to one of his coolly civil greetings, or met the indifferent arrogance in his dark eyes, she thought perhaps she had invented the whole thing out of her own hidden longings. And yet the bruises on her mouth which she had had to disguise with cosmetics had been no mental fabrication. They had been real enough, and she had been afraid Spiro would notice and ask embarrassing questions. But if he was aware of the swollen contours of her mouth, he neither commented nor teased, and she was able to relax and enjoy her dinner.

The taverna he had taken her to was built on a concrete platform which jutted out over the water, and coloured lights clustered in the sheltering olive trees around its perimeter. They had eaten anchovies, and tiny fritters of green pepper and aubergine, and chunks of lamb, roasted with herbs. Later, lingering over coffee and liqueurs, they had watched a string of lighted fishing boats making their way over the tranquil waters.

Under Spiro's guidance, Harriet had learned to appreciate fully the simplicities of Greek taverna food, and to enjoy being invited into the kitchens to see what was being prepared rather than merely consult a written menu.

'It's very different to the food at the villa,' she had commented once, and Spiro had laughed.

'Alex's chef was imported from France,' he had pointed out, and she had smiled back, reflecting ruefully that of course she should have known.

The villa always ran efficiently, but when Alex was there, there was an extra spark in the air, and standards generally peaked past their already high level. He stalked through his domain, never missing a detail, his every wish obeyed instantly, although Harriet had never heard him raise his voice. In every area of life, he expected compliance, and probably got it, she thought with a trace of bitterness. Even Androula scuttled around with vinegary smiles when he was around.

She had braced herself for the pain of seeing him with Maria—of perhaps watching him wooing her, but at least she had been spared that. He was no more attentive to her than any host might have been expected to be with a guest, and although Maria smiled and pouted and beguiled whenever he was near, Harriet had once or twice surprised a faintly chagrined expression on the other girl's face.

Perhaps she had expected pretty speeches, but if a marriage was being arranged between them it would be on his terms and not hers, Harriet told herself with unwonted cynicism.

Meanwhile all Alex's smiles, and any pretty speeches that were going, were being devoted to Nicky. Since his arrival at the villa, he had hardly allowed the child out of his sight, playing with him, spoiling him, carrying him off on his shoulders while Nicky shouted with excitement.

He was deliberately setting out to win him over, Harriet thought with a pang, and that meant her days on Corfu were numbered.

There were no more formal playtimes with Madame Marcos. Alex was there too, and the whole atmosphere was happier, more relaxed. Without ceremony Alex picked Nicky up, putting him on to his mother's lap, into her arms, and Harriet turned away, blaming herself for being over-emotional as she saw the older woman's face soften tremulously into pleasure.

Even Maria had the good sense to keep her real thoughts to herself, and cooed and gushed whenever Nicky was in the vicinity.

Yet something told Harriet that Madame Constantis still had not accepted that Nicky was now part of the household. Her attitude left Harriet feeling both worried and bewildered in a way she could hardly define. On the surface all seemed well. She even treated Harriet herself with courtesy, if not actual enthusiasm, and raised no overt objections to her going out with Spiro.

Yet even this was wrong, Harriet felt intuitively. Madame Constantis was ambitious for her son, and Harriet was sure she hadn't totally abandoned her plans to match him with Maria Xandreou. So why didn't she exert her considerable authority to prevent him making dates with Harriet, and encourage him to flatter Maria with his attentions in the face of Alex's continued indifference? Why did she pretend she didn't mind, because Harriet was ready to swear that she minded like blazes, and she would have given a great deal to know what was going on behind the acid smiles and the blank shuttered eyes.

Particularly where Nicky was concerned. Harriet had never seen Madame Constantis address him directly, or even look at him unless she was obliged to, and her sister's softening towards the little boy had made no difference in her attitude. If anything Harriet sensed a hardening, and additional tension—but it was only a feeling, and when she herself was so much on edge, it was fatally easy to read too much into atmosphere.

Spiro had told her that his mother possessed an apartment in Athens and a large house in the Peloponnese, to which she could return whenever she wished, and Harriet could only hope for Nicky's sake that it would be soon.

She could understand that Madame Marcos and her sister should wish to cling to each other's companionship in their widowhood, but surely the advent of her only grandchild had altered the need for such a dependency? Perhaps Madame Constantis sensed this, and resented it, because there was resentment, and Harriet knew it, although she couldn't prove it.

Harriet sighed and changed her position slightly on her lounger, but not too much because she had cautiously undone the top of her bikini to allow her back to tan evenly. Alex and Spiro had gone fishing and Nicky had gone with his grandmother to visit some friends so she had the beach to herself.

She rested her cheek on her folded arms, feeling the drops of sweat trickling down her forehead, and in the cleft between her breasts. The sky seemed to be clamped over everything like a great brazen lid, and she wondered incuriously whether there was going to be a storm. The air seemed to have that brooding quality about it which a storm might clear. At least she hoped so.

Only hopes, she thought. No certainties—about anything.

She wondered what would happen when she got back to London. That was where she would go, of course. Alex probably wouldn't remember he had guaranteed her employment after she left Corfu, and she had no intention of reminding him. In fact it would be much better if he forgot all about her existence, and she tried to forget about his.

She sighed silently, thinking how much better even than that it would have been if she had never seen him. She was in for a period of great unhappiness, and there seemed no way she could avoid it. How many nights would it take before she could fall asleep without remembering that last merciless pressure of his mouth against hers, and without hungering for his arms to hold her again even if it was anger rather than passion which prompted him?

She pressed her fist against her mouth. It was never likely to be passion. 'Go to Spiro', he had said, and his attitude since had merely underlined his total indifference to her.

She could hear the sound of the boat's engine. They were coming back, and she didn't want to face anyone at the moment. She considered beating a hasty retreat up the path, then opted for pretending to be asleep, closing her eyes and steadying her constricted breathing to a quiet rhythm.

She heard the engine roar to a stop and men's voices speaking in Greek, some laughter. They were approaching, walking up the beach and she felt a mass of tensions, and had to make herself relax.

But when the first cool drops descended on her back, she could maintain the pretence no longer, her eyes flying open as she propped herself up slightly and looked over her shoulder.

She had assumed it was Spiro, perhaps with a handful of seawater, but it was Alex, and he was holding her bottle of sun lotion in his hand. As their eyes met, he crouched lithely beside her and again she felt that delicious coolness on her warm skin, and realised that he was using the lotion on her. She moved restively.

'Keep still,' he ordered. 'It's a fool's trick to fall asleep in the sun. You could have been badly burned.'

She was burning now. As his hand stroked across her flesh, tiny fires were igniting all over her. And as his fingers moved downwards and began to apply the lotion to her lower spine and the gentle curve of her hips above her line of her bikini briefs, she had to sink her teeth into the soft flesh inside her lower lip to prevent herself from crying out.

Oh dear, what kind of a state was she in, that his lightest touch could produce such pleasure and such pain at the same time? she wondered wildly.

When he had finished and was re-capping the bottle, Harriet murmured an awkward 'Thank you,' avoiding his gaze, aware that her cheeks were hectically flushed. Aware too that Spiro was standing only a few yards away, brows raised as he assimilated what was going on.

Her blush deepened. She said inanely, 'Hello. Did you catch anything?'

'Enough, I think,' he said drily.

Alex had turned, dropping the bottle of lotion on to the sand beside her lounger, and moving away to speak to Andonis, who was unloading the fishing gear from the boat at the small jetty.

Spiro walked across to the lounger and looked down at her. 'So we'll eat at the villa tonight, *ne*?'

'Yes,' she agreed brightly, fixing her eyes on him, rejecting the impulse to look round for Alex.

Spiro grinned at her, and his hand snaked down towards her catching her completely off guard. She had lifted herself on to her elbows, and before she could stop him he had twitched the bra of her bikini away from under her body and walked away with it.

'Spiro!' She sat up, wrapping her arms round her half-naked body. 'Bring that back here at once!'

His grin widened. 'Come and get it, *kougla mou*.' With teasing precision, he hung the strip of material from the branch of a convenient olive tree.

Angry and embarrassed, she hesitated, measuring the distance, and wondering if Spiro intended to allow her to retrieve the bra or whether he would simply make off with it again, forcing her to follow. The thought of perhaps having to chase after him through the gardens with only her hands to cover her had no appeal whatsoever.

She said entreatingly, 'Spiro—please?' and heard him laugh tauntingly.

Alex's shadow fell over her. She glanced up at him, her heart thudding with sudden apprehension as she registered the cold rage in his face. He looked almost murderous as he glared at Spiro, snarling something at him in Greek.

For a moment Harriet thought Spiro was going to defy his cousin, and she tensed as Alex took one long stride towards him, then Spiro shrugged almost ruefully, unhooked her top from the branch, and tossed it to him.

Alex turned and almost flung it at her. 'Cover yourself!' he ordered furiously.

She wasn't uncovered. Her folded arms hid more than the few inches of top had ever done, but she sensed that now was not the time to argue, and she turned her back while she fumbled the bra back into place, and fastened its clip.

When she turned back, Alex had gone, but Spiro was still there, gazing up the path with an odd, reflective little smile playing round his mouth.

She said sharply, 'Are you out of your mind? What possessed you to do such a thing?'

'It was an experiment, that is all.' He laughed at the outrage in her face. 'Oh, my poor Harriet, don't look like that! There is no need for you to be angry. Alex has already been angry enough for both of you.'

'I thought he was going to kill you,' she said with a little shiver.

'So did I,' he admitted candidly, and she caught a glimpse of that odd smile again.

Harriet sighed. 'I suppose you know best, Spiro, but as you work for—for your cousin, perhaps it might be better not to—to upset him.'

'I promise not to make a habit of it.' His voice sounded almost lighthearted. 'But perhaps we would be wiser to go without the delicious fresh fish that Alex's chef will be serving tonight, and eat out after all. What do you say?'

She said, 'Yes.' She wasn't hungry. That little incident had deprived her of appetite, but she couldn't bear the thought of encountering Alex again in that mood, and letting Spiro take her to dinner would be the best way she knew of avoiding him.

He had no reason to look at her like that—with such a blaze of contempt in his eyes, she thought stormily, particularly when only minutes before he had been putting lotion on her back, and presumably quite well aware that she wasn't wearing her top.

He operates a hell of a double standard, she thought fuming, wondering how many girls he had seen not merely topless but totally nude. And what would he

have done if she'd been one of the confident beauties
she'd seen parading at Dassia and Sidari on some of her
trips with Spiro? Probably exactly the same, she
acknowledged with a sigh.

She collected her things together and went slowly up
to the villa. She found Nicky in his room, and he
welcomed her with an exuberant hug and a kiss sticky
with lemonade and honey, and she stayed with him
while he had his evening meal, unwinding as she
listened to his excited and not always intelligible
chatter. He was a bright child, and each day he seemed
to pick up more Greek words. By the time he went to
school, he would probably be bi-lingual, and farther
apart from her than any distance could ever achieve.
She had to treasure these moments when she was alone
with him, because his new family were beginning to
close him in with them, and there was no place for her
in that small tight circle of wealth and power.

She bathed Nicky herself that evening, and he
squealed and splashed with all the old delight as they
played once familiar games under Yannina's benevo-
lently smiling gaze. As she wrapped the bath sheet
round his small dripping body, Harriet held him very
close for a moment, aware of a terrible tightness in her
throat, as if she was already saying goodbye to him.
The moment he began to struggle a little, alarmed by
the confining pressure of her arms, she let him go,
tickling him through the folds of towel, and playing
'Round and round the garden' and 'This little piggy'
until he relapsed into his usual happy giggles.

She sat by his bed, waiting for him to fall asleep, and
only when his eyelids had finally drooped did she
relinquish her post and go to her own room to get ready
for her dinner with Spiro.

She had replenished her small wardrobe in Corfu
town, buying several of the inexpensive cotton dresses
falling in masses of pleats from a brief crocheted yoke,
but tonight she decided to wear one of the few dresses
she had bought that she hadn't put on before. It was a

favourite of hers, and she supposed she'd been saving it
for some special occasion. Well, tonight was probably
going to be about as special as she was likely to get, she
thought, throwing it across the bed. It was made from
fine floating Indian cotton in shades of blue and gold,
full-skirted and wide-sleeved. The bodice fitted closely,
and the deeply slashed neckline was fastened at the
throat and halfway to her breasts with delicate blue
cords, finished off with tiny gilded tassels.

It was a romantic dress, a dress for a girl with happy
dreams in her eyes—not the look of strain that she
could disguise behind dark glasses during the daytime,
but which made her totally vulnerable when evening
came.

She applied her make-up with a light hand—a
dusting of shadow for her eyelids, and the merest touch
of colour on her mouth. The natural glow which the
sun had bestowed on her skin needed no extra
embellishment.

She had intended to wear her hair up in a coil, or at
least tied back, but at the last minute she decided to
leave it loose on her shoulders.

She was spraying scent on to her throat and wrists
when there was an abrupt knock on the door and
Androula came in.

'I'm asked to say the car is at the door, *thespinis*.' Her
voice was as unfriendly as her face.

Harriet swallowed as the woman's gaze flickered
disapprovingly over her. 'Please tell the *kyrios* that I'll
be down right away.'

Androula nodded silently and vanished.

Harriet gave herself a last searching look, decided it
was all the best she could do, and started downstairs.
Halfway along the corridor she met Madame
Constantis. She was surprised to see her, as the older
woman's room was in a different part of the house, and
she had rarely encountered her on the upper floor.

She glanced at Zoe Constantis, expecting the acid
twitch of the lips which passed for a smile with her, but

not even that was forthcoming. The look which reached her from under the heavy lids was pure venom—no longer even a pretence at friendliness and acceptance, and Harriet almost recoiled physically as if an actual blow had been aimed at her. She glanced back over her shoulder as she reached the corner, watching the thin upright figure move out of sight, like some kind of ancient Fury in her black dress, and had to pause for a moment to try and recover her composure.

She had never been wholly convinced about Madame Constantis' apparent change of attitude towards her, but she hadn't expected to have her suspicions so blightingly confirmed either.

Not for the first time, she wondered how such a grim woman could ever have given birth to such a pleasant easy-going son as Spiro.

The car was parked just outside the circle of light which spilled from the villa's open doors, and as Harriet crossed towards it, she heard in the distance the first rumble of thunder. It seemed the storm she had predicted was on its way.

The passenger door was already open, and she slipped into her seat, tucking her skirt protectively away from the door before she closed it. The engine was already running, she realised, purring like some big cat. Spiro was in a hurry to be off. Perhaps he had also had an encounter with his mother, and wanted to escape.

She said with a little gasp as the car moved forward, 'I'm sorry I'm late. I've been putting Nicky to bed and . . .' Her voice stopped abruptly, as she turned and looked at her companion for the first time.

Alex smiled sardonically at the frank shock in her eyes. 'And as always, Harriet *mou*, you are worth waiting for.'

'What are you doing here?' she demanded heatedly. 'Where is Spiro?'

'On his way back to Athens. His holiday is over for a while.'

For a moment she was unable to speak, then she said,

'Was that really necessary? What happened on the beach was only a joke, after all.'

His laugh had a bite to it. 'You flatter yourself Spiro's tasteless horseplay has no connection with his departure. A minor problem has developed in the Athens office which I hope he can deal with before it blows up into a minor crisis, that is all. I am sorry he did not have time to explain in person, or say goodbye to you in the manner you would wish.'

'There's no need for that.' Her voice was stiff. 'A simple message telling me that the evening was off would have been sufficient.'

'But you're my guest, Harriet *mou*,' he said silkily 'And a good host would not allow you to be deprived of an evening's pleasure when it is in his power to fill the inevitable void which Spiro's departure must create.'

'That's very kind of you,' she said woodenly. 'But I'd really prefer to go back to the villa, if you don't mind.'

'But I do mind,' he retorted. The car seemed to leap forward and Harriet, who had been fumbling with the catch on her seatbelt for no very coherent reason, sank back in her seat with a gasp. 'Tonight you are having dinner with me.'

'And my wishes don't matter, I suppose.' She stared down at her hands clamped rigidly together in her lap.

'On this occasion, no. We have things to discuss. Harriet, and privacy at my home is not always easy to achieve.'

She smoothed a fold of her dress. 'I—see. I suppose you want to talk about Nicky—and when I'm going home.'

'Those are among the topics we shall be considering,' he said drily. 'Or did you imagine that life was going to pursue its present course indefinitely?'

'Of course not.' She kept her head bent. 'As a matter of fact, I think Nicky's settled down amazingly well. I'm quite ready to leave whenever you say the word. There's—just one thing.' She paused, biting her lip.

You've spent a lot of time with him lately. I think he's going to feel rather bereft—when you're away such a great deal. He might find the periods of separation easier to take, if you didn't pay him quite so much attention.'

He said coldly, 'I have no intention of being separated from Nicky for long periods, at least until he is old enough to go to school.'

She was taken aback. 'But you can hardly trail him round the world in your wake with a nursemaid in tow,' she protested. 'What kind of security is that?'

His brows lifted. 'Nicos will be with my wife, and my wife will be with me. A child's true security does not lie within four walls as much as in the love and warmth of those who care for him. We shall be his home.'

Harriet wanted to ask bitterly, 'Have you discussed this with Maria, and established her point of view?' But it seemed safer to remain silent. His words suggested that he wasn't entering marriage quite as cynically as Spiro had indicated. In fact they created a curiously intimate picture, considering he didn't appear to be in love with Maria. But then, she thought, Alex had always taken his responsibilities to the Marcos Corporation very seriously. Why should she imagine he would adopt a different attitude to his eventual marriage? Even the most dedicated playboy must surely tire of that kind of existence in the end.

'You are very quiet,' he said. 'Does my explanation not satisfy you?'

'It's—perfectly satisfactory.' She swallowed painfully. 'I—I hope you'll be very happy.'

'Do you, Harriet?' He laughed. 'I had formed the impression you would rather see me boiled in oil.'

'Perhaps so,' she said. 'But that wouldn't be the best thing for Nicky.'

He said, 'His happiness is what matters most to you still, Harriet. Is that not so?'

No, she thought. Heaven help me, it's you that matters most. You matter more to me than anything in my life.

She said quietly, 'That's right.' She hesitated. 'I'm glad that your mother is—well—beginning. . . .'

'You need not struggle for words. I know what you are trying to say, and I am also glad. I had begun to wonder if she would ever be able to reconcile her need for Nicos with the unhappy memories his arrival was bound to revive.'

She bit her lip. 'You don't have to hedge round the subject, Alex. Spiro told me what was supposed to have happened.'

There was a silence, then in a voice shaken with anger Alex said, 'He had no right. . . .'

'I persuaded him,' she interrupted. 'I made him tell me. I had to know—for Nicky's sake. You must see that.' She paused, then added, 'And I don't believe a word of it.'

He said evenly, 'You are hardly in a position to say that. You were not here at the time.'

'I didn't have to be. I knew Kostas too. I never knew him to do anything mean or despicable, and I can't understand why—as his brother—you should have been so ready to condemn him.'

Alex pulled on the wheel, swerving the car off the road on to the verge beneath some trees, and stopping the engine.

'Is that what you think, Harriet? How little you know! Condemning Kostas, as you put it, was the hardest decision I have ever made. Yes, it was out of character for him to do such a thing, but that night he was not himself. He was more angry than I had ever seen him. He had quarrelled with our mother most bitterly. He had demanded the ring from her, and when she refused——' he shrugged, 'I can only presume he decided to take the law into his own hands. When I found the safe it had been rifled—every box had been opened, but only the ring had gone. That and the documents which had provided him with an excuse for going to the safe in the first place,' he added grimly.

'I don't care.' Stubbornly Harriet shook her head. 'I

still won't believe it. If he felt he was entitled to this ring for Becca, then why didn't he give it to her?'

His glance was cynical. 'He did not?'

'No!' she almost exploded.

He shrugged. 'A belated sense of shame, perhaps. Perhaps he honoured your sister by believing she would not be ready to ally herself with someone who would stoop to steal from his own family. Or would she?' His tone sharpened.

'Of course not,' she said wretchedly. 'The very least idea, and Becca would have had a fit!'

'My mother, of course, believes that he stole the ring at her urging.'

'So Spiro said. And that isn't true either. Becca may not have been the heiress your mother wanted for her son, but she was no gold-digger.' She glared at him. 'But I see now why you were so ready to offer me money to give up Nicky. You thought that we were—tarred with the same brush.'

'What do you want of me?' Alex asked softly. 'An insincere denial? Or my assurance that it is some time since I have speculated in those terms about either you or your late sister?'

'I don't give a damn what you think,' she said shakily. 'But if that's how it was, then why the hell did you bring me here?'

He said, 'I think you know why.'

His hands reached for her, lifting her bodily towards him out of her seat with an irresistible force. He turned her harshly so that she lay across his body, helpless in the crook of his arm, her eyes dilating with mingled alarm and excitement as his head came down towards her. He began to kiss her, lightly at first, the merest brushing of his mouth against her cheekbones, her temples and her startled eyes. When at last his lips took hers, it was in a kind of agony, as if he was dying, and she was an elixir that could bring him to life. Her mouth parted of its own volition and blind instinct took over, prompting a response as fierce and pagan as his

own demand of her. Her hands locked tightly behind
his head, drawing him down to her, holding him close.
The touch of him, the taste of him was a sensual
enslavement, and her body arched towards him in a
silent offering of utter completeness.

He began to caress her, his fingers stroking her
hair, then moving down to her throat and the soft
sensitive hollows beneath her ears. His fingers were
gentle, but they brought every nerve-ending to raw,
aching life.

She heard herself whimper against his lips, but it was
with pleasure, not protest, as he tugged open the little
blue cords, and his hand slid under the soft cling of her
neckline in intimate exploration. Her whole body
seemed to clench as his thumb stroked delicately across
the budding rose of her nipple, sending shafts of white-
hot sensation through the very core of her being.

Nothing seemed to exist in the world but the heat of
his body enfolding her, the warm draining languor of
his mouth, and the sheer scorch of pleasure that his
slow expert caresses were creating for her.

Her breath shuddered in her throat as he lifted his
mouth from hers at last, pressing featherlight kisses
down the smooth flesh of her neck to the curve of her
shoulder. His lips brushed the soft veil of material away
from her breasts, and her body was convulsed in
yearning as his mouth took possession of the aroused
rosy peaks, the insistent flick of his tongue against her
flesh increasing her excitement almost to the point of
frenzy.

She was touching him in her turn, her hands sliding
over his body without inhibition, discovering the
warmth of his skin, the play of muscle beneath the
elegant clothes.

She was hungry for him as if, starved all her life, she
had suddenly been offered a banquet. She loved Alex,
and wanted him, and the need to tell him so was slowly
overwhelming her.

Her lips moved to speak his name, but instead she

cried out, frightened, because the whole world was
suddenly enveloped in blue-white light, and as the
darkness rolled back, an immense crack of thunder
exploded around them. And with the thunder came
rain, drumming on the roof and splashing the
windscreen.

Alex lifted himself away from her with evident
reluctance, to close the window at his side. Harriet
huddled back into her own seat, thankful that the
shadows concealed her burning face. The shock of the
lightning had restored her to a kind of shamed sanity,
and she fumbled with her dress fastenings as she
struggled for composure.

She had let him hold her, kiss her, explore her body
with his hands and mouth when only a short while
before he had spoken openly about his forthcoming
marriage. A sense of decency at least should have made
her fight him, reject his caresses, she thought, feeling
sick.

The window adjusted to his satisfaction, he turned to
her, and she spoke in a small strained voice. 'Will you
take me back to the villa, please.'

He said slowly, 'The storm will pass. And we are
supposed to be having dinner.'

'I hate storms. I'm terrified of them.' She certainly
sounded as if she was, she thought detachedly. Her
voice was almost cracking. 'Nicky hates them too, and
I want to make sure he's all right. And I don't want any
dinner. I—I couldn't eat anything,' she ended on a little
rush of words.

'Well, that at least may be true,' he said, his voice
hardening with contempt. 'I seem to have lost my
appetite—for food—myself. As for your fear of storms,
Harriet *mou*,—you're not a physical coward, merely a
moral one. Yet you need not have worried. Seducing
inexperienced girls in cars is a callow trick which has
never appealed to me.'

The car engine started with a roar, and he turned the
vehicle with almost savage expertise, and sent them

rocketing back the way they had come, while the thunder growled and rumbled above their heads.

As he drew up at the entrance, Alex said with scarcely controlled impatience, 'Do you wish to wait here while I fetch some covering—an umbrella, perhaps?'

'N-no,' Harriet stammered. 'I'll be fine, honestly.'

'Honestly?' he echoed. 'I doubt if you know the meaning of the word. You had better run, then.'

Run she did, head bent, not glancing behind to see if he was following. She took the stairs two at a time, and went straight to Nicky's room. It was quite true, he hated storms—when he was awake. But it was extremely doubtful if the thunder would have woken him.

His door was standing ajar, which surprised her. Perhaps he had woken after all, and Yannina was with him, she thought, as she stopped inside.

But there was no comforting figure at Nicky's bedside, and the bed itself was empty.

Harriet stood very still, lower lip caught in her teeth, while she registered this.

She walked over to the baby alarm above the bed, and saw it was switched off. She turned it on and said, 'Yannina—is Nicky with you?' Then she sank down on the bedside chair and waited, trying not to panic.

It seemed a long time later, but it was actually only seconds, that feet came flying down the passage and Yannina burst into the room, her startled gaze seeking the empty bed. The expression on her face told Harriet all she needed to know.

She said carefully, 'It's all right, Yannina. He probably woke and was frightened by the storm and went downstairs.'

Yannina's eyes were round. 'But the handle on the door, *thespinis*. It is too high, and too stiff for him to manage, as you yourself know well. How could he have left the room? You did not leave the door open.'

No, thought Harriet, and the alarm was switched on, because I checked it as I always do.

She tried to smile. 'Well, someone came in—perhaps his grandmother—and took him downstairs because he was frightened.'

Nicky had never been a wakeful child at nights, nor a wanderer, she told herself. He was probably downstairs at this moment being fed titbits in the dining room.

She said, 'I'll go and check.'

She ran out of the room full tilt into Alex. He caught her by the arms steadying her, his eyes sharpening.

'What is it?' he demanded. 'Are you ill?'

'No.' She tried to steady her breathing. 'Is—is Nicky downstairs? Have you seen him?'

'No to both questions.' His fingers tightened on her arms until she could have cried out. 'What are you saying?'

Her voice was toneless. 'He's not in his room, and Yannina hasn't seen him. His door was open and someone had switched off the alarm.'

There was a greyish tinge suddenly under the swarthy skin as he stared at her. He reached out and gripped the door jamb for a moment as if he needed support, and beneath his breath he whispered something that might have been a prayer or an oath in Greek.

He looked at her grimly. 'I'll get a search going. Look in his room again—look in the bathroom in case he's hiding. You say the door was open. What about the window?'

For a moment she felt sick, then she said, 'No—the shutters were fastened,' and saw the relief on his face.

She searched as he'd told her, but Nicky wasn't hiding. If he had been, he would have come out when he heard their voices, she knew, unless he was too frightened. . . .

Frightened of what? The storm? Or something else?

She stood in the middle of the room, listening to the rapid sounds of activity elsewhere in the villa. So many rooms, so many places where a little boy could be lost, a child whom she had left sleeping deeply and safely.

Her palms were damp suddenly, and she wiped them mechanically on her floating skirt. She didn't like a single one of the thoughts that were beginning to press on her mind, but they had to be faced somehow.

With a new purpose she went out of the room, and towards the stairs. Alex was in the hall, and he looked up as she came towards him, his face taut. 'Well?'

She shook her head. 'No sign. I'm going to look outside.'

'He won't have gone out there,' he said with conviction. 'It is still pouring with rain, and you said he was frightened of storms.'

'Perhaps the storm hadn't started when he was taken out there,' she said.

'Taken?' The look sharpened to a glare, and his brown cheeks flushed ominously. 'Are you suggesting that someone in this house would do such a thing? Why?'

'Probably because he's his father's son,' Harriet said levelly. 'Or hasn't it ever occurred to you that someone got rid of Kostas too?'

She went past him and out into the rain and the darkness.

CHAPTER TEN

SHE was drenched to the skin within minutes, the thin cotton clinging uncomfortably round her limbs. Rain had made the paths slippery and she walked fast, but with care, pausing every few minutes to call, 'Nicky!'

As she reached the swimming pool, all the lights round it went on as if Alex, from the house, had guessed the route she had taken. She had to make herself look into the water, but the pool was empty except for the toy swan floating rather forlornly in the shallow end. Harriet bit her lip and hurried on.

The gate down to the beach stood wide. The ground seemed to fall away in front of her like a descent into hell, and she wished she had brought a flashlight, but there was not time to fetch one now. She slipped off her sandals and began to make her way slowly and painfully down the path, catching at shrubs and the branches of trees to steady her progress.

In the end she nearly fell over him. He was lying in a little crumpled heap at the side of the path, and she fell on her knees, touching him frantically, terribly afraid. The path was awash, and children older than Nicky had drowned in puddles before this. The relief when she felt his shallow breathing under her hands, and heard the slight moan he gave as she turned him, was enormous. He was soaked and cold, however, and next door to unconscious with a sizeable bump on his forehead, she discovered, her fingertips tenderly exploring. He might have other injuries—perhaps she shouldn't move him.

Above her on the path she heard the slither of other footsteps, and she flung back her head and almost screamed Alex's name, because it could be anyone coming down towards them in the darkness.

Alex said, 'Hush, *agape mou*. I am here.' He lifted her

161

gently to her feet, and she clung to him, her hands fierce
with panic, her breath sobbing harshly in her throat.
There were other people behind him—Andonis, she
saw, and Yannina, her face twisted with anxiety.

She felt Alex's mouth brush her wet hair. He said,
'We must get him to the house. Can you walk or shall I
help you?'

She disengaged herself from him, embarrassment
taking the place of relief in her emotions. She had flung
herself at him as if he was her hope of salvation.

'I can manage,' she muttered, averting her face.

Madame Marcos was standing in the hall as they
all trooped in, Andonis carrying Nicky cradled
protectively against his broad chest. She looked
terrible, the usually immaculate coiffure dishevelled as
if she had been clawing at it. Her hands were tearing
at a lace-edged handkerchief. She started forward
with a little cry, her face agonised, and Alex put a
swiftly protective arm round her, speaking soothingly
in his own language.

There was something strange and dreamlike about
the whole scene, Harriet thought dazedly. In the
distance she could hear the last growls of thunder as the
storm finally retreated, and closer at hand above the
splash of the rain through the open door, came the
sound of a woman wailing and distraught.

She knew who it was. The hall was full of people,
concerned, chattering and staring. Even Maria was
there, her eyes nearly popping out of her head. There was
only one person missing—the woman whose ambition
for her son had been so disastrously underestimated. By
all of us, Harriet thought numbly, remembering her
own secret amusement as she'd watched Zoe Constantis
trying to push Spiro and Maria together. And yet in her
heart, surely she had always known that the older
woman was no laughing matter. . . .

Alex was beside her. He said, 'The doctor is on his
way.'

Her voice sounded far away. She said, 'That's good.

That's very good,' and the world tilted and slid slowly
away.

The doctor was young and stocky with a heavy black
moustache. In perfect but accented English he assured
Harriet that her fainting fit had been caused by stress
after the unfortunate events of the evening, and that
sleep would soon restore her. This was the conclusion
she had already drawn herself, but it was reassuring to
have it confirmed.

She felt a fraud anyway, because once she had
regained consciousness, and got out of her wet clothes
and into a warm bath, she had begun to feel better
almost at once. The chicken broth that a very subdued,
red-eyed Androula had brought her had helped too,
because, quite apart from anything else, she realised,
she'd been *hungry*.

The doctor had calmed some of her fears about
Nicky too. He had suffered other bumps and
contusions as a result of his fall, but there were no broken
bones, and he was only slightly concussed. Pneumonia
was always a danger, but with care he felt it could be
averted. He spoke with a certain amount of constraint,
and Harriet guessed he was also thinking about the
other patient he had been called to that evening.
Presumably he had administered some kind of sedative,
because the dreadful, spine-chilling wailing had stopped
now.

'He is a strong healthy child, *thespinis*.' The doctor
rose to leave. 'But it is a fortunate thing that he was
found no later.' He smiled at her kindly. 'Although he
was not born on the island, already our saint has him in
his care. No harm will come to him now.'

It was a consoling thought, Harriet found, as she lay
back against her pillows, agreeing meekly that it would
be better for her to remain where she was rather than
take a turn at sitting up with Nicky.

He asked her if he should leave her some tablets to
help her sleep, but she refused. She felt exhausted,

waves of tiredness seemed to be beating at her. She would have no trouble in sleeping, she told herself.

Nor did she. The trouble came in her dreams, dark, swamping confusions where everyone seemed her enemy, and she ran endlessly down black tunnels with Nicky in her arms, trying to escape the hatred which stalked behind. She was saying a name, crying it hysterically because the darkness was clamping round her, and this time he would not rescue her in time. It was like another miracle when his arms closed round her, lifting her up into light and safety and a warmth that made her bones ache.

She opened dazed eyes. She was lying wrapped in Alex's arms, her face buried into the curve of his throat.

With a stifled gasp she pulled herself away, out of his embrace.

'What are you doing here?'

'I came to make sure you were all right.' His voice was husky. 'You seemed to be having a nightmare, and I tried to comfort you. I did not mean to wake you. I'm sorry.'

She stared at him, shaken and incredulous. He wasn't actually in bed with her, just lying on top of it next to her, and that was bad enough.

She said, 'I'd hardly be likely to go on sleeping in the circumstances.'

His mouth twisted slightly. 'No? You did that night in London.' After a long, taut pause while she endeavoured to make sense of what he had just said, he added, 'You called my name then, too.'

She remembered that night, those dreams, the odd sense of loss in the morning when she had woken alone. Her voice sounded strangled. 'You—slept with me?'

'*You* slept, *agape mou*.' Propped on one elbow, he looked at her wryly. 'I spent an uncomfortable night fighting my conscience—and losing. I have cursed myself for being a fool a hundred times since then.'

'Don't!' Harriet pressed her hands against her burning face.

'Little hypocrite,' he said, amused. 'Are you really trying to pretend you do not know that I want you? And if I tell you that I know you want me too, will you call me names again?'

There was little point in denying it, she thought, staring down at the scalloped edge of the sheet she was clutching as if it was her shield and defender. Was it really only a few hours earlier that Alex had stirred her to that frenzied response? It seemed like a lifetime ago.

He talks about wanting, she thought. Not about love.

She said dully, 'No, I won't call you names. And I was—having a nightmare. I didn't realise I was making a noise.'

'Why should you?' he asked coolly. 'And don't sound apologetic, Harriet *mou*. After what has transpired in this house, you are entitled to a nightmare or two.'

She said in a muffled voice, 'I'm so sorry. It's so awful. Do you know why . . .?'

'Oh, yes.' The amusement vanished. He sounded tired and a little defeated. 'She had decided a long time ago that Spiro should be my heir. After Kostas, he was my nearest male relative. Perhaps you guessed?' She nodded. He went on, 'From speaking to my mother earlier, I gather that—my aunt encouraged the original rift between them and that when Kostas returned, she seized the opportunity to do him more harm. When he visited the safe, he was in too much of a temper to secure it properly, and she waited until the room was empty and then took the ring herself. It has been with her ever since, at the bottom of the bag in which she keeps her tapestries and threads,' he added with a kind of groan. 'My poor mother is shattered, as you can imagine. She has always known that Thia Zoe was envious because she felt my mother made a better marriage, but that her own sister could behave in such a way—cause her such agony—is beyond belief. And of course if my mother ever showed signs of softening towards Kostas, Thia Zoe was there, reminding her of the "wrong" he had done her.' He said something short and savage in his own language.

After a pause, he went on, 'Before Nicos ever came here she tried to turn my mother against him, by hinting that he might not be Kostas' child. She cited the indiscreet behaviour that some girls from England and other parts of Europe are guilty of when they come to Corfu, and said that your sister would share the same easy morals. She tried every way to turn my mother against the boy—but you probably know this?'

'I think I sensed it,' Harriet said. 'But there was nothing tangible. I knew she disliked me too, yet she seemed quite amenable when Spiro began taking me out, even though. . . .' She stopped abruptly.

'Even though what?'

She was flushing again. 'Even though she was trying to get Spiro to pay attention to Maria.'

'She intended Spiro to seduce you,' he said in a matter-of-fact tone. 'If he had done so, she would have used this as an excuse to have you sent away. She wished you to be sent back to England, because you were too close to Nicos, too protective. She has admitted this. She had convinced herself that I would never marry—and that with Nicos gone, that her son, or at least her grandson, would inherit the Marcos Corporation.' He paused, then said flatly, 'She knows better now.'

He meant that he was going to be married, she thought. She felt sick and dead inside, but she forced her voice to be as casual as his had been.

'Then why did she choose tonight . . .?'

'She is a sick woman. The news that Spiro had been sent to Athens—servants' gossip that it was because of you that he had been sent away must have finally unbalanced her. Androula had told her that we were out together, so she would have assumed that she was safe for several hours. Only—we came back.'

Harriet said, 'Yes.' Then, 'What are you going to do?'

'She cannot remain here. But to initiate any official intervention would cause a scandal, hurting many people. Instead I have decided it will be best if she returns to her house in the Peloponnese and remains there. Spiro of course will have to be told.' His mouth tightened. 'A task I do not relish.'

There were tears on her face suddenly. 'Poor Spiro!'

'Lucky Spiro,' he said grimly. 'When he has you to weep for him.'

He pulled her into his arms, his mouth hard on hers, and Harriet responded, her lips parting achingly, feverishly beneath the onslaught of his. Her body clung to his as if she had been magnetised, her arms winding round his neck in passionate abandon. All the doubts, the barriers she had imposed melted and dissolved as his kiss deepened. Alex turned her in his arms, his warm weight pressing her down into the softness of the mattress while his urgent mouth plundered kisses from her throat and shoulders.

His fingers slid aside the straps of her nightgown. He said gently, 'You do not need this, *agape mou*. Tonight you will wear only my kisses.'

She did not have time to feel shy. He had already unfastened the two decorous buttons that closed the bodice, and the gentle slide of his hands down her body as he uncovered her was a bewitchment in itself. But when it was done, and she was naked in his arms, she closed her eyes, a little afraid of the hunger she saw as he looked at her.

He said softly, 'Scared of me, *matia mou*! There is no need. If you want no more of me than this, I will hold you until you fall asleep.' He paused. 'Tell me which it is to be, my beautiful one, sleep or love.'

She couldn't say the word. It meant too much to her, while to him it was only a physical act. Instead she reached up, drawing him down to her, his mouth to hers, his hands to her breasts, and heard his hoarse sigh of pleasure against her lips.

The hunger was controlled like a leashed tiger as he aroused her gently, but with passionate skill. Loving him as she did, her compliance to his desire was ensured, but she soon learned he wanted more than that. Under his tender, sensuous tutelage she became mindless, rapturously acceptant as each new intimacy was unfolded to her, until at last there were no more secrets left.

Her body moved with his in a rhythm which bordered on savagery, the first confusion of pain and delight receding until only the pleasure was left, and she moaned aloud, her head falling back on the pillow as waves of sensation broke over her.

Alex kissed her, stroking the softness of her parted lips, and murmured to her in his own language. Harriet lay in his arms, dazed and trembling with joy. She pressed her mouth against the warmth of his shoulder, and stroked his face with her fingertips. She was lost for words, but that didn't seem to matter when touching and kissing seemed to say so much more.

Later they showered together, and she stood in the protective circle of his arms as the cool water cascaded over them.

She thought, 'It's not true, none of it can be true, and soon the door will open and someone will bring in breakfast and it will all have been a dream.'

Alex switched off the water. He said, 'You sigh, *agape mou.* Have I made you sad?'

She shook her head. 'I didn't know I could be so happy,' she confessed.

'Nor I.' His voice was quiet, almost reflective.

He wrapped her in one of the bath-sheets and carried her back to bed, his mouth warm and urgent against her body.

A long time later, a lifetime later, she opened her eyes. Alex was standing by the window, wearing his robe. As she stirred and sat up, he turned and smiled at her.

'*Kalimera,*' he said softly. 'Do you know how beautiful you are?'

Her face warmed, but with pleasure, not embarrassment. She was no longer shy when his dark arrogant gaze explored her body, instead she gloried in it.

She put out a hand to him. She said softly, 'It's lonely here.'

Alex groaned. 'You must not tempt me, my lovely one. It is almost light, and the servants will be moving around soon. You would not wish me to be found in your room.'

'I shouldn't mind.'

'Well, I should,' he said, the dark face suddenly austere. 'You must know as well as I do, Harriet, that this should not have happened.'

She felt cold suddenly, and hitched the sheet closer round her body. She said huskily, 'You're sorry that it did?'

'No.' His voice was impatient. 'How could I regret anything so—perfect, yet I did not intend. . . .' He paused, pushing a hand through his dark hair in a weary, slightly irritable gesture. 'I have to leave you now, Harriet, but later we must talk. You realise that?'

He came over to the bed and bending down kissed her mouth briefly and not too gently. She put her arms round his neck, wanting to draw him down to her, to hold him, to recapture even for a few minutes the passion and the tenderness they had shared, but Alex disengaged himself firmly.

'No,' he grated, and left her.

She was so cold now, she was shaking with it, huddling back against the pillows. With daylight, reality had come indeed, and it frightened her. She shivered. Last night had been the most precious experience of her life, but she had to face the fact that for Alex it could not have been the same, that for him she might simply have been one more girl in one more bed.

Oh no! she thought, pressing her fist against her trembling mouth. Alex was a sexual expert, he knew everything there was to know about women's bodies, how to gauge every kiss, every caress and intimacy in order to gain the response he wanted. And she had been no different. He had known she was a virgin, and the gentleness, the almost superhuman control he had shown while he was arousing her need not have been because he cared about her, but simply a means to an end, because he knew that in the end his restraint would reap its own reward.

As it had, she told herself numbly. She had never dreamed she was capable of such fevered, agonised passion, or that such heights of pleasure existed, let alone could be scaled.

Naïvely, she had seen Alex's possession of her as a beginning, but it could well be the opposite. All the old-fashioned laws about self-respect, about holding a man at arms' length in order to keep his interest, were coming back to haunt her. She had given Alex her body without reticence, loved him without holding back, presented him, in fact, with everything he wanted from her without ever questioning if it might be all he wanted.

In those dark hours of rapture, he had never once spoken of love, she realised unhappily. Loving had been her own connotation. His might be very different—no more than the gratification of a need.

Hurt clenched inside her. If Alex had stayed with her, she thought frantically, if she had woken up in his arms, warmed by his kisses she wouldn't be thinking like this. Yet he couldn't wait to get out of her room.

She turned over on to her stomach, convulsively burying her face in the pillow, trying to hold pain at bay. He had said that they would talk later, and perhaps then she would receive the reassurance she craved.

After a while she fell asleep, and when she next opened her eyes, the room was alive with sunlight, and Androula had brought in her breakfast. Harriet thanked her quietly, feeling selfconscious when the woman bent and retrieved her nightgown, still lying in a little crumpled heap on the floor where Alex had tossed it, and placed it expressionlessly on the bed.

She showered and dressed after she had drunk some

coffee, and left her room, intending to visit Nicky. But Androula was waiting for her in the corridor.

'Kyria Marcos wishes to speak to you, *thespinis*. She is waiting for you in the study.'

Harriet paused, frankly surprised, although she had expected there would be some sort of interview with Nicky's grandmother some time during the day.

She said slowly, 'But I was going to see Nicos. . . .'

'The doctor is with him, *thespinis*. And Kyria Marcos is waiting for you—now.' Androula was practically barring her way, and short of using force, Harriet couldn't see any way of getting past her. She wasn't looking forward to seeing Madame Marcos. It was going to be deeply embarrassing and difficult to discuss what had happened to Nicky when the person who had tried to harm him—who had inflicted such damage in the past—was Madame's own sister. Harriet would have to choose her words carefully.

Androula went with her, accompanying her to the study door, and even knocking and opening it for her. It was almost like being in custody, Harriet thought with a slight inner grimace.

The room was shuttered and dim, and Madame was seated behind a large polished desk. She was very still, her hands folded in her lap, and her face, although ravaged, looked calm.

She said, 'I have to thank you, Miss Masters. I understand it was because of you that my grandson's peril was so quickly discovered.'

She spoke of thanks, but there was little evident gratitude in her face as she looked at Harriet, no warmth in the dark eyes. But then Harriet thought wryly, wasn't that just what she'd expected in the circumstances?

She said, 'You don't need to say any more, Madame. I love Nicky.'

'Yes, I am sure that you do.' Madame Marcos made a sudden restless movement. 'However, I am also sure that when you first came here, it was made clear that it could not be a permanent arrangement.'

Harriet felt herself tense into rigidity. She said, 'Yes—quite clear. Are—are you asking me to leave?'

'I think it is time that you did. Now that you are my son's mistress, you are hardly an appropriate companion for Nicos. You imagined I did not know?' she added harshly, as Harriet gasped and colour flared in her face. 'Do not attempt to deny it. I saw Alex with my own eyes going back to his own room this morning. I spoke with him before he left and he admitted he had spent the night with you.'

'Before—he left?' Harriet repeated, the words stinging her brain. 'You mean he isn't here?'

Madame Marcos said heavily, 'He is—escorting his aunt to her house in the Peloponnese.' Her tone sharpened. 'You look ill, Miss Masters. Perhaps you had better sit down. Clearly you have been cherishing some illusions about Alex's intentions towards you. Perhaps you even hoped to emulate your sister and contract a marriage within our family.' She shook her head. 'If so, you made a grave mistake. Alex will marry Maria Xandreou in the New Year.' She paused, studying Harriet gravely. 'He has been at fault in his behaviour towards you, *thespinis*, but——' she shrugged, 'he is very much a man, and you are an attractive girl. Alex has always taken and enjoyed whatever life has had to offer. But you must understand that your presence in this house, for Maria's sake, and for other reasons as well, is now an embarrassment, and it would be best for all of us if you were to leave.'

She hesitated again, then said levelly, 'If your—arrangement with my son had been a long-term one he would no doubt have made some financial provision for you. He is not ungenerous in such matters. As it is, I am to give you this.' She produced a long flat case, and pushed it across the desk towards Harriet.

A piece of jewellery, Harriet thought, staring at it numbly. The ultimate insult. She wanted to say something, but she could not make her voice work.

Madame Marcos was continuing. A seat had been

obtained for her on a plane to Athens, and another booking made from Athens to London. A maid would be sent to assist with her packing.

At last she found words. 'Am I—am I going to be allowed to say goodbye to Nicky?'

Madame Marcos' mouth tightened. 'Of course. We are not inhuman, Miss Masters, and you, I think are not a fool. You must have known that this—indelicate situation could not continue.'

Harriet sank her teeth into her lower lip. 'Yes,' she said tonelessly.

'I was certain you would be sensible.' Madame Marcos touched the box. 'You have forgotten your bracelet.'

'Is that what it is?' Harriet threw her head back. 'I haven't forgotten it. I just don't share your family's obsession with jewellery—the giving of it, or the withholding of it. Keep the bracelet for the next lady. After all, Alex is hardly likely to remain celibate until the New Year.' She sent the box sliding contemptuously back towards the older woman across the polished surface of the desk, and walked out.

She paused for a moment in the hall outside, struggling to maintain her composure, while a voice whispered crazily in her head, 'So that's it. Over. Finished.'

She wanted to cry and scream, but that was impossible. She didn't know how Alex's discarded women usually behaved, but she needed to salvage some rags of dignity, if she could.

One day, some day, perhaps she would be glad that he didn't know the truth, that she hadn't blurted out her love for him, but not yet. All she was aware of now was an emptiness as big as the world as she walked very slowly up the stairs to Nicky's room.

CHAPTER ELEVEN

HARRIET felt dispirited as she made her way back to Manda's house. The temporary job she had had since her return to London had ended that day, and the agency had nothing else for her at the moment. She felt ridiculously disappointed, because she had had every reason to believe that the temp job had been about to become a permanency. Roger Clayton who ran the office had spoken enthusiastically about her work, and a possible vacancy, but today he had simply shaken hands with her and muttered something about her efficiency.

At least she now had some money, she thought, and she could pay Manda and Bill something for allowing her to stay with them. They had been endlessly kind since she had arrived pale and hollow-eyed on their doorstep, insisting that she could stay as long as she needed to.

Harriet had been determined that it should only be a short stay. She had to pick up her life and go on. Her job with her old company had gone, of course, but the personnel department had taken her address and telephone number and promised they would be in touch if a new opportunity came up. So far, she had heard nothing, and she had begun to doubt if she ever would, so it wasn't yet feasible to start searching for a bed-sitter of her own again without a steady job to pay for it.

The children Manda was minding had all gone home, and Manda was sitting at the kitchen table with a freshly brewed pot of coffee in front of her as Harriet let herself in at the back door.

Manda smiled across at her. 'Well?'

Harriet shook her head. 'Ill,' she returned with an

effort at lightness. 'It's the dole next week, I'm afraid.
Which reminds me——' She delved into her bag and
produced her wage envelope.

'Keep it,' said Manda. 'You're airing the spare room
for us, after all, and heaven knows, you don't eat
enough to keep a fly alive.'

Harriet flushed slightly. Manda was a good cook,
and it must have gone hard with her to sit opposite a
guest who sat picking at her dinner most evenings. She
had told Manda just enough to convince her that it
would have been impossible for her to have stayed at
the villa, without going into details over her involvement
with Alex, and hoped they would interpret her general
wanness and lack of appetite as pining for Nicky. But
she had often intercepted a shrewd look from Manda and
thought helplessly that her friend wasn't deceived for a
minute, although she asked no embarrassing questions.

She said quietly, 'I'd rather pay my way—while I
can.'

'Jobs with liveable wages are hard to come by,'
Manda agreed. She poured coffee into a cup and
pushed it across the table to Harriet. She went on
reflectively, 'Of course you could always contact the
Marcos Corporation and remind them that you only
went to Corfu on the promise of a job when you
returned.'

Harriet's flush deepened. She said, 'I'd rather die.'

'I thought so somehow,' Manda murmured, smiling
into her own cup.

Harriet sighed abruptly. 'What do you want to
know?' It might even be a relief to confide in someone,
she thought.

Manda shrugged. 'What do I need to know?' she
countered. 'You don't eat, and you don't sleep. Half the
time you walk round in a dream. Nicky's a lovely child,
but I can't believe he's had this profound effect.'

'No, he hasn't.' Harriet bit her lip. 'Although I miss
him terribly. I—I worry about him too. He was still
half-asleep when I saw him, and he started telling me

something about "the witch". He could have nightmares for years about it all—or he could be ill.'

'I doubt it.' Manda patted her arm reassuringly, as Harriet's voice shook. 'Children are resilient little beasts, and everything that happened that night will probably just seem like a bad dream to him soon. It was hardly the psychological moment to get you to leave, though,' she added, her brow creased.

Harriet forced a smile. 'Oh, I don't know. I've had time to think since, and I believe in some ways Madame Marcos almost blamed me for what happened. I think she felt it was my presence which had pushed Madame Constantis to do as she did.'

'In other words, she'd rather have gone on sharing her home with a nut-case than learn the truth?' Manda questioned. She shook her head. 'I'll accept that you might have reminded her of things she'd rather pretend never happened, but so will Nicky, for heaven's sake, and she kept him. Drink your coffee,' she added prosaically.

Harriet obeyed shakily. After a pause, she said, 'You're right, of course. That was only part of it. She wanted to be rid of me because I was involved with— Alex.' She still found it hard to say his name.

Manda said carefully, 'When you say involved. . . .'

Harriet stared concentratedly into her cup as if she was trying to analyse the contents. 'That's exactly what I mean.'

'That's what I was afraid of,' Manda muttered, and gave an exasperated sigh.

'All right.' Harriet spread her hands defensively. 'Tell me what a fool I've been.'

Manda's mouth curved humorously. 'I'd say you know that already. Isn't that what you've been telling yourself night after night, walking up and down in your room? No, I haven't been listening at the door,' she added with a slight grimace. 'But I had to get up for the twins one night, and I saw your light on. I was afraid you might be ill.' She paused and said with unmistakable emphasis, 'You're not, are you?'

'No,' Harriet said tautly. 'No—I don't even have that.' It was something that had occurred to her once the first agony of her departure was over, that a new life could have been created from that one glorious night in Alex's arms. But she knew now that it was not to be.

'Don't talk like that,' Manda reproached. 'You know quite well from Nicky that bringing up a child singlehanded is no picnic. Even when the father is alive and well able to provide the financial support,' she added.

Harriet bent her head unhappily. 'I know. I know all that, but I still hoped. That's the sort of fool I've been.'

'Hell's bells,' Manda said helplessly. There was a long silence, then she said gently, 'Does he know how you feel?'

Harriet shook her head, and Manda's lips tightened. 'Well, he must have been an insensitive bastard.'

'No.' Harriet was instantly defensive. 'I was careful never to let him guess.'

'While you were having a full-blooded affair?' Manda demanded sceptically. 'What did you do—tell him it was just your little hobby?'

'Hardly,' Harriet sighed. 'I don't think he'd have believed me. And it was a very short-lived affair,' she added with wry bitterness. 'One night, to be exact. Hardly a basis for declarations of undying love.'

'And certainly nothing to ruin the rest of your life for,' Manda told her.

She was right, and Harriet knew it. Those last few hours on Corfu had been full of forlorn hopes—that Alex would return by some miracle and prevent her from leaving, even that he'd snatch her off the plane before it could take off. But by the time she had waited at Athens for her connection, and endured the flight to London, a sober, more realistic train of thought had intervened. Alex wanted her to leave. His mother had only been carrying out his wishes. Her only hope of salvation was to forget him, to put everything that had happened out of her mind, no matter how long it took.

And if it meant cutting herself off from Nicky, then she would have to do that too, however much it hurt.

She'd heard a saying once, 'Love makes time pass. Time makes love pass.' Well, when time had done its work, perhaps one day she could make contact again, all passion spent. He would be married, of course. She might even be married too, although nothing seemed less likely.

She spent the weekend studying newspapers for possible jobs, and writing endless letters of application for anything that seemed of interest, not just in the capital, but all over the country. A change of scene might be what she needed, she thought.

On Monday it rained, and she spent a depressing day going the rounds of more temp agencies, getting her name on their books. Everywhere there seemed to be retrenchment, and she wasn't offered much, apart from a week's audio typing in ten days' time. It was late afternoon by the time she made her way back to Manda's feeling a little footsore, and wondering rather fatalistically if she would ever have a regular job again. . . .

She was walking up the path, when the door opened and Manda leapt out at her, a child in her arms and two more clinging to her long skirt.

'Thank heavens you're back!' she exclaimed. 'That Greek's been on the telephone. Oh, honey, not him,' she added woefully, as she took in Harriet's sudden tautness. 'The other one—Mr Philippides.'

'But how did he know where I was?' Harriet demanded.

'Search me. But he wants you to go to his office as soon as possible. It's something about Nicky.' Manda's eyes looked compassionately at Harriet's paling cheeks. 'He said it was pretty urgent, but he wouldn't go into details.'

Harriet's mouth trembled. 'There was a chance—just a chance of pneumonia. Oh, Manda, do you think . . .?'

'I don't know what to think, except that you'd better

do as he asks and get over there right away. He's left his number, so that I can phone and tell him you're on your way.'

Harriet lingered. 'Perhaps if I phoned he'd tell me. . . .'

'Go on!' Manda gave her a little push. 'If by any remote chance it is an emergency, he may want you to go with him somewhere. What about your passport? Have you got that?'

'It's in my bag.' Harriet felt sick. Nicky, she thought, ill—or worse. Nicky calling for her. It might already be too late. 'I'll go at once.'

'I'd come with you,' said Manda, 'only——' she gestured expressively at her small hangers-on. 'Will you let me know—whatever the news?'

'Of course I will.' Tiredness forgotten, Harriet began to run back the way she had come.

The journey seemed endless. She began to wonder what time Mr Philippides' office closed, and whether she would arrive in time. It would be torture if it was all shut up, and she had to go back to Manda's and wait on tenterhooks until the following day. She splurged on a taxi for the last few miles, and sat on the edge of her seat nervously watching the traffic, silently cursing every hold-up. Her destination reached, she thrust some money into the driver's hand after a cursory glance at the meter, and ran breathlessly up the steps. The commissionaire swung the door open, and by some miracle there was a lift waiting at the ground floor.

Outside the door to Mr Philippides' suite of offices, she paused and took one or two steadying breaths.

He stood up as she was shown into his room, with a welcoming smile that she did not feel capable of returning.

She said hoarsely, 'Nicky—what's happened to him?'

'Miss Masters—*thespinis*—sit down. Let me order my secretary to bring you some coffee.'

She moistened her dry mouth with the tip of her tongue. 'I don't want coffee, I just want to know about

Nicky. Please—I've come all this way. You must tell me!'

His face was compassionate as he looked at her. 'All in good time, dear young lady. But first that coffee.'

He went past her into the outer room, and Harriet buried her face in her hands with a little groan. If he really felt so strongly that she would need a stimulant, it had to be bad news.

She heard the door re-open, and looked up, summoning all her courage.

Alex stood watching her, his dark face set in grim, accusing lines.

Her lips parted in a soundless gasp. Then she whispered pleadingly, 'Nicky?'

'Apart from missing you, he is perfectly well,' he said harshly.

'Then—why the message?' It was so hard to speak, she felt as if she was using someone else's voice.

His mouth twisted sardonically. 'If I had said it was myself who wished to see you, would you have come?' He saw her flinch, and the dark brows drew together. 'I thought not.'

'You used Nicky,' she accused. 'How could you?'

He gestured impatiently. 'Nicky is at my hotel at this very moment. I assumed you would wish to see him. Was I wrong?'

Harriet shook her head.

'Then you shall,' he said almost conversationally. 'For a price.'

She lifted her head and stared at him, her face revealing her sense of shock. Her mouth moved slowly. 'What price?'

Alex gave a short angry laugh. 'Not what you seem to think. Just a talk—the one you cheated me of when you left Corfu so precipitately.'

She looked away. 'I think everything has been said already.'

'Well, I do not. Show me your hands, Harriet *mou*.'

She hesitated. 'I don't understand—why . . .?'

'Don't argue with me.' His voice softened danger-
ously. 'Just show me your hands.'

Mutely she extended them, palms upwards. He took
them in his, his fingers closing in a painful grip, turning
them over, his eyes flicking over the slim, ringless
fingers.

He said, 'So you are not engaged, or married yet.'

She pulled her hands away, hating the deep aching
need that his lightest touch could engender. 'No, of
course not.'

'Then what has gone wrong? Is it possible you
confessed something to your lover which has made
him have second thoughts? Perhaps a dowry might
sweeten him?' He reached in his pocket and drew out
a flat jeweller's case. Harriet recognised it at once. He
flicked it open and tossed it into her lap. The
sapphires and diamonds in the bracelet glittered
coldly at her. He said smoothly, 'I hope this will
compensate your fiancé for the loss of his—virgin
bride.'

She shivered, pushing at the box with unsteady hands
so that it slid off her lap on to the carpeted floor. 'I
don't want it.'

'Ah,' he said, bitterly mocking. 'You wanted
something better, perhaps. My mother's ruby ring, for
example.'

'Manda was right,' she said unevenly. 'You are an
insensitive bastard, Alex.'

'I advise you not to call me names. Since you left me,
I have had time and leisure to think of a few for you,'
he said bleakly.

'I don't want to hear them.' Harriet stood up. 'If the
talk you spoke of was just to give you another
opportunity to insult me with this——' she touched the
bracelet with the toe of her shoe—'then I'd rather not
hear any more of that, either.'

'Perhaps you had better consult your future husband
before you reject such a valuable gift.'

'I have no future husband,' she said stormily. 'Yes,

I'd like to see Nicky, but if it means I have to be tormented by you, Alex, then I'll go home instead.'

He stared at her. 'Spiro told me there was a man in England. He said he had it from your own lips even though you had denied it to me. When you ran out on me, I told myself it could only be to return to him.'

'Yes, I told Spiro something of the sort,' she admitted wearily. 'But only to stop him getting any ideas.'

'You were afraid he might make love to you.' He shook his head. 'He would not have done so.'

'What makes you so sure?'

He bit his lip. 'Because he knew that I wanted you for myself.'

'And nothing must stand in the way of what you want. That's right, isn't it, Alex? And nothing did, because you had me. Or have you forgotten?'

'No,' Alex said softly. 'I have forgotten nothing.'

The look in his eyes brought her to her feet. Harriet said hoarsely, 'Don't come near me! Don't touch me, or I'll scream the place down!'

He sighed impatiently. 'Harriet *mou*. You are in the London offices of the Marcos Corporation. You might scream your head off, but no one would come to your assistance, even if I were to rape you here on the carpet.' He paused. 'Except that we both know it would not be rape.'

She turned towards the door, aware that her pulses were hammering tumultuously and afraid that by some sensual perception he would know it too. She said quietly, 'I would like to go now, please. Give—give Nicky my love when you see him.'

Before she could reach the door he was at her side, his hand closing round her arm with a grip that hurt. 'You may give him your message yourself,' said Alex with a smile which did not reach his eyes.

'Let go of me!' she panted.

'Struggle or make a scene, and I will carry you down to the car,' he warned, and he was totally serious, she knew.

The place seemed deserted, but Harriet knew that was only an illusion. There were dozens of pairs of eyes watching them all the way to the lift, then across the foyer to the door and the car beyond. Alex's grip on her arm didn't relax by so much as an iota as he steered her down the steps and into the car.

She said huskily, 'This is an outrage!'

'You think so? Wait until you discover my plans for the remainder of the evening.'

He was actually laughing at her, she thought furiously, not deigning him a reply or even a glance, as she sat rigidly staring out of the window.

It was no real surprise to find the hotel suite empty, but she felt panic rising within her just the same.

She said, 'You lied to me.'

'I told you the truth. Nicky is in fact in the adjoining suite with my mother. We shall be joining her for dinner later. You may see him then.'

She drew a sharp breath. 'Dinner with your mother? Are you insane?'

He gave her a faint smile. 'I don't think so, Harriet *mou*. You are thinking perhaps of the last time you spoke to my mother. But then, you see, she was suffering from a misapprehension—several of them, in fact.'

She said faintly, 'I don't understand.'

Alex waved her to one of the sofas. 'Sit down and I will explain. My mother has a godchild to whom she feels a strong sense of duty. A few years ago she tried to arrange a marriage between the girl and my brother Kostas, and you know what became of that. So instead my mother got it fixed in her head that Maria and I would make each other happy. It has taken me a long time to convince her that the man capable of enduring Maria and her tantrums probably does not exist on this planet, but at last she believes me.'

It was very quiet in the suite. Harriet's hands were clasped together so tightly that the knuckles showed white.

'Her second misapprehension concerned you, *agape mou*. As you know, I did not want the servants to see me leaving your bedroom. What I did not bargain for was that Mama had been sitting up with Nicos and was on her way back to her own room to rest. She saw me. She was very angry, as you can imagine. She has few illusions about me, but I have never made a habit of seducing girls under the roof she shares with me. When she confronted me that morning there was little I could say in my defence. Besides, she was in a highly charged emotional state over—Thia Zoe. It seemed wiser to say as little as possible. But I did let her know that you were not merely a casual sexual fling.'

He sighed, then said flatly, 'This worried her. She had lost Kostas to your sister. She was afraid that she would lose me to you, so she decided to send you away, and use the bracelet she knew I had brought you from Athens as some kind of—kiss-off payment.' He paused. 'When I found you'd gone, and she admitted what she had done, I could not believe it. You see, *agape mou*, I had convinced myself that you were in love with me, and it seemed impossible that you should have given credence to what she had told you and just—left. I thought that you would have contacted me somehow, if not from the villa then at least when you changed planes at Athens, and asked for an explanation, or told me where you were going—an address—something. If Philippides had not happened to call the firm you used to work for, who told him where you were staying, it might have been weeks before I found you.'

Harriet stared down at a minute fleck on one of her nails as if mesmerised by it. She could not speak.

Alex went on, 'And then Spiro told me reluctantly about this man you had mentioned, and it seemed to explain why there had been no message—not even a word of goodbye. I felt sick to my stomach, so I took myself to Athens and got very drunk.'

She found her voice. 'And your mistress in Athens? What about her?'

'Spiro again,' he said savagely. 'No, Harriet, I did not visit Penelope. I had already said goodbye to her on a previous occasion. She knew from the start of our relationship that it would end as soon as I met the woman I intended to marry.'

'Poor Penelope! Did you get her a bracelet too?'

He swore. 'No, I did not! I bought your bracelet, not as a farewell, but to fasten round your wrist when I asked you to marry me, you little fool!'

She said slowly, 'You—wanted to marry me?'

'Why do you speak as if it is in the past?' he asked impatiently. 'Yes, I want to marry you. Why else should I be here? I told myself that this man could not mean anything to you, that if he had, you could not have surrendered to me as you did, my sweet one.'

He took a step towards her, and she shrank back against the cushions. 'Don't come near me!'

For a moment he stared at her, then he gave a slight shrug and sat down at the other end of the sofa. Perversely, Harriet was disappointed. She needed to keep a clear head, and if he touched her again, she would melt, she would die, but on the other hand she desperately needed him to take her in his arms and kiss away all the doubts, unhappiness and sheer panic which were making her wretched.

He had said he was not going to marry Maria, that he intended to marry her, and she could have been dazzled by that—except that there still had been no word of love.

That was what she had to remember. And that he had said he thought she loved him, which meant he was probably convinced she would fall into his arms without question.

She asked steadily, 'Why do you want to marry me? For—Nicky's sake?'

He smiled. 'It would solve many problems, as I am sure you agree.'

She bit her lip. 'And that's all?' she asked tautly.

The smile widened, and his dark eyes moved

lingeringly over her body. 'Why, no,' he said softly. 'Perhaps—also—to give my child a name.'

'I'm not pregnant,' she snapped, and he threw back his head and laughed.

'But then you still have not heard my plans for the remainder of the evening, *agape mou.*'

'And I'm not going to bed with you either.' She was back on the defensive again.

He lifted his brows. 'No? Then it will prove a very frustrating marriage for us both.'

Harriet snatched up her bag and got to her feet, her heart thudding painfully. 'There'll be no marriage,' she said. 'You—you've had the talk you wanted, so please may I go now.'

Alex was beside her as she reached the door. He twisted the strap of her bag from her fingers and tossed it aside, then picked her up in his arms and carried her effortlessly across the room to a door that could only lead to a bedroom. Harriet kicked and squirmed furiously, but he didn't even seem to notice. He stopped suddenly, and his mouth came down on hers in a fierce relentless kiss that seemed to go on for ever. Then he dropped her, winded and breathless, in the very centre of the kingsize bed.

Harriet lay, looking up at him, her eyes enormous as he shrugged out of his elegant jacket and tugged off his tie. As he began to unbutton his shirt, she rolled away from him across the bed, but he was too quick for her, dragging her back ruthlessly, and kneeling astride her, pinioning her between his thighs to control her angry struggles.

'If you touch me, you'll be sorry!' she spat at him.

'If I do not touch you, we shall both be sorry.' He pulled off his shirt and tossed it on to the floor, and his hand was caressing her, tracing the curve of her face, the line of her jaw and throat, until her body seemed one silent scream of pain and longing.

She tried to hit him, and he took both her wrists in one hand and held them above her head while he started to undress her. His mouth sought hers, but she turned her head away sharply in rejection, so he began to kiss her body instead, the warm seduction of his lips and tongue on her skin arousing a fever in her blood which was soon raging out of control.

She could fight him at a distance, but when she was lying in his arms like this, his lips and fingers moving over her in an exploration of heart-stopping intimacy, then she was fighting herself, all her deepest and most secret needs and cravings.

He released her wrists and her hands cradled his head, her fingers tangling in the thickness of his dark hair, her palms sliding smoothly over the planes and angles of his face.

Alex lifted himself away from her, staring down at her, his dark eyes hungry and intent. 'Now tell me you don't want me,' he said between his teeth.

Pain was like a stone in her throat. She said, 'But wanting isn't love, Alex. And it takes love to make a marriage.'

He was silent and very still for a moment, and then he sighed, a deep shuddering breath that seemed to shake his whole body.

He said in a dry, bleak voice, 'Was I wrong, then? But if this——' his hand touched her bare breast like a kiss '—and this—is all there is, then it is enough for a beginning, Harriet *mou*. Oh, my sweet one, I can teach you to need me in all the other ways, to trust me. Don't leave me again, my precious heart. Stay with me. I can make you love me.'

Hope was unfurling deep inside her like the petals of some strange, exotic flower.

On a whisper, she said, 'You—love me?'

He said huskily, 'Almost from the first, *agape mou*. How could you not know?'

'How could I?' she protested. That inner radiance was spreading, glowing in her face and eyes, curving her mouth. 'Why didn't you tell me?'

'Did it need words? And at first, I admit, I tried to

fight it. There had been Kostas—and it seemed there would always be too many obstacles, too many barriers between us. But you were in my heart, *matia mou*, almost before I knew it.'

He bent and kissed her, his mouth tender almost reverent.

Harriet said shyly, 'But you were so cold to me. . . .'

He sighed. 'I thought it was Spiro that you wanted. I came back from Athens half crazy for you. I'd intended to suggest that you take that cruise I mentioned—but with me instead of alone, and then I saw you with Spiro and it was like a knife in the guts.'

She stroked his cheek. 'He was only being kind. I think he knew I needed a friend.'

'I did not always appreciate his brand of friendship,' he said grimly. 'That day on the beach, for example, I was ready to kill him. I gave myself away completely. His first words to me afterwards were, "So you have been caught at last, cousin".'

'You did rather overreact.' She smiled at him. 'Poor Spiro! He's had a very rough time lately. We must be kind to him.'

'But not too kind,' Alex threatened mockingly, then sobered. 'Yes, he has been shocked and grieved beyond words, but he recognises now that his mother is a sick woman.' He paused. 'And I have made sure there is extra work, extra responsibility to keep his mind occupied.'

'And your mother?' she asked quietly. 'How have you managed to reconcile her?'

'I will not pretend it has been easy, but she is a determined woman, *agape mou*, not a heartless one. But for Thia Zoe's intervention I think she would eventually have forgiven Kostas and welcomed your sister. Now she has learned a lesson. She is not prepared to make the same mistake with me, and that is why she came to London with me—to make amends to you, to prove she is prepared to accept you as my wife.' He looked into her eyes. 'Tell me that you will marry me, Harriet, my dear love.'

Her hands stroked the strength of his naked shoulders, and moved provocatively down his back. A laugh quivered in her voice. 'It isn't exactly a conventional proposal, but I think I could be persuaded—Alex *mou*.'

He said huskily, 'Then I shall lose no time in persuading you.'

His lips took hers in warm possession, and her arms closed round him, her body yielding and eager, accepting love, accepting all life had to offer in her share of paradise with Alex.

Harlequin® Plus

HARLEQUIN'S YORKSHIRE PUDDING

Harriet, Alex and Nicky sit down to a traditional English dinner of roast beef and Yorkshire pudding. Next time you serve your family or friends roast beef, try substituting our delicious and simple recipe for Yorkshire pudding for the traditional North American roast potatoes!

What you need:
(to serve 10-12)

2 eggs (extra large)
1 cup all-purpose flour
½ tsp. salt
1½ cups milk
10-12 tbsp. of beef dripping, butter or margarine

What to do:

Approximately 3 hours before serving time, beat eggs in a large bowl. Add flour and salt and blend. Add milk gradually, combining thoroughly. Resulting mixture should cling like thick cream to the back of a spoon. Refrigerate for at least 2 hours.

About 30 minutes before serving time, heat oven to 450°F (230°C). Pour one tbsp. of beef dripping into each cavity of a muffin pan and heat in oven for 5 minutes. Remove mixture from refrigerator and pour quickly into heated muffin pan, filling each cavity about ⅔ full. Place in oven and bake 20-25 minutes, until puddings are puffed and browned.